SALMON BEACH
The Narrows Camps

by

Royal LaPlante

BLACK FOREST PRESS
San Diego, California
October 2003
First Edition

SALMON BEACH
The Narrows Camps

by

Royal LaPlante

PUBLISHED IN THE UNITED STATES OF AMERICA
BY
BLACK FOREST PRESS
P.O. Box 6342
Chula Vista, CA 91909-6342
1-800-451-9404

Other Novels by Royal LaPlante:

THE MYRTLEWOOD GROVE 1994 AND 1998

MYRTLEWOOD GROVE REVISTED 1999

MYRTLEWOOD GROVE FINAL EPISODE 2000

PENALOMAH, THE EAGLE SOARS 1997

COTTAGE COVE,
A CHECHACO IN ALASKA 1998 AND 1999

UNCLE JACK'S CREEK 1999

Disclaimer

Printed in the United States of America
Library of Congress
Cataloging-in-Publication

ISBN: 1-58275-031-9

Dedication

In memorial to Margaret Louise Shannon LaPlante, her family dedicates this story of early Salmon Beach. To her husband Royal Anthony LaPlante, she was a devoted and loving wife, as well as a dedicated mother to their daughter Betty Louise LaPlante Larson and their son Royal Anthony LaPlante, Junior. To everyone she was their friend Maggie or Margaret.

During her twenty-seven years as a widow she became the matriarch of her expanding family of two children, six grandchildren, eleven great-grandchildren, and one great-great-grandchild. Her gentle wisdom and sympathetic ear endeared her to family, neighbors and friends.

The gracious lady working in her yard around the red house near the corner of Browns Point Boulevard and McMurray Road will forever remain in the memory of her loved ones.

Acknowledgments

The author acknowledges the meticulous preparation and editing of this manuscript by Lynette Splinter and the proofreading by her mother, Barbara Splinter. As with all his novels, his wife Joanne has provided support, ideas and encouragement.

Special thanks are offered to Dahk Knox, Mary Inbody and Glenna Jacket of Black Forest Press for excellent advice and assistance in publishing this book.

The contributions of local historian Roger Edwards of Salmon Beach were significant. His research files, photographs and maps provided historical and anecdotal integrity to this tale of the South Sound.

Prologue

The skinny boy was perched atop a piling along the busy dock, observing the activities as the *Kalequah* approached. The packet was making its weekly rounds of the South Sound, and Captain Trilby waved to the lad. His brown eyes were lively with curiosity even while his dusky-skinned countenance remained stoically without expression. He brushed a non-existent wisp of hair from his forehead, remembering after the fact that his teacher had cut his long black hair only yesterday – the last day of school.

Harry also recalled his arrival at the Point Fosdick Reservation last fall, delivered by Captain Trilby in his packet under the guardianship of a Puyallup Tribal Elder following the drowning death of his fisherman father just two days before. His tears had shamed him that day, but he had not cried since. Actually he liked his new home and school well enough, most people seeming like his family here on the reservation.

A young Nisqually girl stood at the boat's railing, a stooped old man beside her reminiscent of his own guardian last year. The Nisqually Elder appeared unattached to his charge, merely performing a required duty somewhat begrudgingly. The pretty girl with dark brown hair, shadowed eyes and wearing a simple sackcloth dress of indeterminate color, shyly waved to the watching lad. He surprised himself by returning a like gesture of friendship. Maybe a sister is what he needed in his lonely orphan's life.

Having committed himself to being amiable, Harry slid off his perch and walked across the scarred planking to offer his help in carrying her two bundles.

"I'm Annie from the Nisqually River. Momma died last week. I'm new here."

Nodding with understanding and compassion, Harry

replied, "I'm Harry from the Puyallup River and I'm an orphan, too. It's not so bad here. School's fun and fishing is good."

Captain Trilby called out the wheelhouse window in a congenial voice, "Harry! You take care of Annie. She's a good girl."

Harry waved in agreement, the two new friends walking side-by-side up the lane to the federal office, where the taciturn Nisqually man handed over Annie and a legal document to the clerk, returning hastily to the waiting *Kahlequah* with nary a word spoken.

Harry planned to show his new friend around despite teasing from the boys in his dormitory. Comradeship transcended any personal discomfort. Annie needed him and Harry felt responsibility for her welfare. Besides, he was a Puyallup and could whip any of the Nisquallies in his class.

Chapter 1

The still-green farmlands of North Dakota stretched across the plains endlessly, broken here and there by a rounded hill or shallow ditch. Before a red barn nearby, the stooped figure of an old farmer coaxed his sweaty gray mare in wrenching a bleached and twisted entanglement of roots from the ground. The slow-motion action passed from view as the Northern Pacific train sped westerly, soon coming upon a team of two brown nags pulling a clapboard wagon loaded with a family of eight and a pile of supplies.

Probably headed home after a big day on that town back there, the young man mused as he continued viewing the monotonous panorama from his car window. Jim Gerber slouched in the hard seat with eyelids drooping, giving his clear blue eyes an uncharacteristically mean look. A straight shock of recently clipped hair hung over his forehead, its unremarkable light brown color matching the day's growth of facial hair. Both traits were inherited from his mother although Augusta Gerber had turned gray when his father had died five years ago.

Jim's beach stocking cap lay upon his well-worn canvas seaman's bag at his feet, which were encased in brown leather half-boots with matching laces. Brand new Levis were cinched at the waist by a black belt sporting a rather large brass buckle shaped like a tugboat – a parting gift from his captain. Completing his outfit was a red and brown plaid shirt covered by an open tan jacket with brass buttons and two breast pockets. His rail ticket protruded from one and a railroad time schedule from the other.

After almost two days on the train out of Philadelphia, Jim's attention wandered, his thoughts returning to Chicago, *Golly, I'll be eighteen years old in a couple of weeks and I looked like a green-*

horn yesterday when I was robbed. How could I be so careless that moment after being so cautious all day?

I decided to use the layover time to see the streets of Chicago. Ha! I didn't even get off the train before that big fellow backed into me instead of stepping onto the platform, and then that nice-hmph-lady fell into my arms and held on while I helped her onto her feet. They were both gone when I realized my wallet was missing. I looked for it around the car door for several minutes before the conductor asked me what I was doing. Hmph, he had a good laugh when I explained my dilemma. I suppose my red-faced expression when he told me I had fallen for a pickpocket's trick got his sympathy. He advised me to chalk it up to experience and stay on the train. I'd be left behind if I filed a report with the ticket agent and Chicago police.

*****

His daydreaming was interrupted by the motherly lady across the aisle, who repeated her question a third time, "Young man, my son and I have bread and cheese left over from our lunch. Would you like it?"

At his hesitation she added, "Robert will sleep all the way home. I wouldn't want it to go to waste."

Jim noticed the conductor was watching them intently and realized two kind souls were conspiring to help him. His sober countenance slowly changed as his infectious grin turned him into a fine-looking fellow, and he replied, "Thank you, Ma'am! I am hungry and your food is gratefully accepted. Didn't I see you two come aboard in Minneapolis?"

"Yes, we were visiting my sister's family for a nice vacation, but I'll be glad to get home to Dickinson. It's just up ahead a few miles. Would you like an apple tart as well?"

The kind lady was rewarded with a broad smile of appreciation, and the conductor was pleased at Jim's wink of recognition for his good deed.

Chatting off and on for the next hour, the conductor's call of "Dickinson!" brought both travelers to their feet simultaneously, the mother waking her boy while Jim unwound his lanky almost-six-foot frame. His gangling legs were well-muscled, and his build was sturdier than it looked at first glance. He had no trouble handling his new friend's bags, placing them on the platform before waving good-bye as the Northern Pacific time schedule was kept and the train chugged away.

Returning to his seat with the clickity-clackety sound in his ears, Jim was pleased to find his melancholy was alleviated and spirits buoyed by the friendly treatment of the travelers, and ruminated, *I feel better. Passing acts of kindness offset the theft by those con artists. That's why I stashed a five-dollar gold piece in my fancy belt buckle – a trick the Captain showed me. Yet I hated to lose my wallet, and I'll miss my family pictures. Oh well, I plan to start a new life out West anyway. Should I choose gold in the Klondike or work boats in the Puget Sound?*

*****

Jim awoke with a start, sated appetite and peace of mind having allowed him to relax with an afternoon nap. The conductor spoke from behind him, "Have a nice sleep? Your seat seems awfully hard for a coast-to-coast trip. My call for Miles City must have startled you, eh?"

Nodding agreeably, the young passenger replied, "Thanks for the information and that kind lady's leftovers. What time is it? I don't own a watch."

"Ha! Ha! And I thought those Chicago thieves stole it. It's just past eight o'clock. It'll be nighttime most of the way to Spokane," his friend replied, adding an afterthought, "After the train leaves Miles City, I'll lead you to the baggage car and a kettle of pork and beans our mailman is cooking."

Jim smiled his appreciation and drifted back into his reverie, nostalgic images of his family dominating his thoughts, *I was*

glad to see Steffi last month. I worried about Harold Allen work-
ing on the farm when Wilhelm went off to fight with Teddy
Roosevelt in Cuba. My sister never had a serious beau before Hal
courted her, and now look at her. Big as a house, with child and
beaming with happiness at the prospect of family life. She married
Hal a short time before our brother was killed on San Juan Hill,
and they moved to Connecticut to live near the Allen family.

She was glad to get away from the farm, I know. We were a
happy family when we were children, popular and charming
Wilhelm devoting himself to his helpless baby brother Gunther
while our eldest brother Hans worked beside father in the fields.
Fortunately the Mongoloid infirmities claimed Gunther before
Father died in 1894 and the Gerber family fell on hard times. Our
small farm near Scranton lay between the Lackawanna River and
the crossroads of Old Forge, and Daddy's labors fed us decently as
well as supplying a little cash for Momma's household.

My father always dreamed of owning a winery, "like the
Graf's kellar in the Nahe valley," but his vines only produced
enough grapes for his homemade wine. Let's see, my folks were
married in Bad Kreuznach in 1872, Herman Kantergerber, the
vintner apprentice, and Augusta Schmidt, the shopkeeper's daugh-
ter. They came to America a year and a half later.

Momma still tells the story of that careless official in the
port of New York, an Italian naturally, who ignored and misunder-
stood the complaints of a German immigrant and changed Daddy's
name to Herman Kantergerber. She laughs as she rattles off the
results of the new family name, Hans Kantergerber, Wilhelm
Kantergerber, Steffi Kantergerber, Gunther Kantergerber, and me,
James Kantergerber.

Oh, those were happy days. I was called "J.K." or "Jakie"
by everyone, but that stopped abruptly when father died. It seems
that nothing was ever the same again. I tried to work with Hans,
but nothing I did satisfied him. Hans was head of our family, but
he was not my father, and he seemed mean and selfish to me – the
youngest brother. Wilhelm was easygoing and popular with every-

one in our grange and the Old Forge Grammar School, even though he was too young for one and too old for the other. Because he was taller than Hans and good with tools, they got along just fine, and Steffi worked with Momma in the house so she avoided my big brother's bad temper.

I still remember my fourteenth birthday party when I was copying Wilhelm's playful antics. I guess teasing Hans was not very nice, but we were having fun when he reached across the dinner table and slapped my face good and hard. His look of hatred hurt more than the blow and silenced my protest.

I glanced toward mother for intervention, a word of rebuke to both of us, but she looked away in confusion. I'm a lot like Hans in the matter of a bad temper, and it erupted in a fit of malice as I tossed the gravy bowl into Hans' face, followed by the mashed potatoes and a glass of milk – plus a few curses.

When Hans pulled his leather belt free of his trousers with a fierce growl and a spoken threat to spank me, I chortled an incomprehensible retort and fisted the carving knife. Wilhelm came between us, and at his loving touch I relaxed and dropped the knife.

"Jakie! You mind Hans if you're going to live in this house," Momma asserted her family role a bit late, for I was stubborn and fixed in my rebellion. I left my home ten minutes later with all my belongings in a burlap potato sack and a pocket full of pennies and one silver quarter, every cent Wilhelm and Steffi could muster.

I walked and worked my way easterly all summer, arriving at Dingman's Ferry on the Delaware River just as the leaves were turning to golden tones. I cut wood for the ferryman and slept in his woodshed until an old-time riverboat pulled into the landing. Toting five cords of firewood across the gangplank earned me a job as stoker for Captain Kane. I had a warm bunk in the boiler room, three meals a day and one dollar a week to spend.

Ha! Ha! The Captain is a wise old man. Made me write Momma on the first of every month and insisted I enclose a few dollars at Christmas. After my bitterness waned, he gave me time off *to visit home in the spring of 1897. I found Wilhelm had moved to Philadelphia and was working in a factory, and Harold Allen was Hans' helper on the farm while he courted Steffi. They seemed very serious about love when I returned to my riverboat job, and an announcement of their wedding came in the mail a few weeks later. It was postmarked New London, Connecticut where the newlyweds had settled. Hal was working for his father in his small boatyard.*

Steffi's letters became my news source for the family, Hans had married Elsa Bucher and the following year baby Herman was born, Wilhelm had gone to Texas and joined Teddy Roosevelt's Rough Riders, Steffi was with child, and then the sad news of Wilhelm's death on San Juan Hill in Cuba. Tear stains covered the page – Steffi's or mine, I can't remember.

"Jim! Come along and we'll sample my friend's supper," the conductor called, leading the young passenger with a rumbling stomach to the baggage car.

*****

Deep purple shadows enshrouded the vast rangelands outside of Billings as Jim joined a bevy of gawking passengers, taking in a scattering of horsemen to the south. A traveling salesman-type in a suit, spats and bowler hat was spouting off, "See those Sioux savages out there. I bet their fathers were at the Little Big Horn shooting at Custer's brave soldiers. Cowardly heathen!"

"Eek! One of those devils is sitting right over there," a middle-aged lady screeched, shaking a finger at an Indian dressed in cowboy garb.

"Ma'am, I'm a Crow like my friends out there, and our fathers scouted for Colonel Custer and Major Reno," the well-spoken young man corrected the blowhard and set the record straight.

The salesman grew red in the face, huffing and puffing, and sensing some support from his fellow passengers, railed at the Crow lad, "You heathen, we should throw you off this train so you can be with those Indians outside. I swear, you…"

"That's enough my friend, Charlie is a Christian and an American, just like you and me. He's my partner," a raggedly dressed old-timer retorted, his weather-beaten face as darkly tanned as that of his Crow friend.

Jim surprised himself when he spoke up, "Reckon he's welcome to share our car. I'm Jim Gerber from Pennsylvania, and I'd like to hear about the Crow Nation."

The small crowd grumbled but returned to their seats as Jim winked at the old-timer, and Charlie replied softly, "Thank you Mister Gerber. You're welcome on our reservation any time, just tell everyone you're a friend of Charlie Gray Eagle."

The veteran cowboy explained, "Those lads are coming into Billings to meet my partner, who is the son of a chief. Charlie is eager to meet them, so we'll be leaving. We just didn't appreciate being pushed. Have a safe trip, Jim Gerber."

Jim returned to his seat under the baleful gaze of the fancy-pants salesman, staring the man down before taking his seat. The screeching lady was braver and not as circumspect, accusatory tones evident as she spoke, "Are you an Indian-lover, young man? What would your mother say?"

Coming erect and stepping forward to the woman's seat, Jim offered respectfully, "Probably she'd react like you Ma'am, and I am sorry you were upset by this situation. Charlie Gray Eagle was minding his own business and didn't deserve to be pestered. Don't you agree?"

Her companion quickly agreed with Jim, telling his wife, "Dear, Mister Gerber is right. That Crow lad was behaving himself. Jim had the courage to say so."

*****

Dozing fretfully during the night, Jim finally stretched his muscles by climbing to his feet and walking the aisle. He noticed only a few seats were occupied and ambled into the next coach to find scarcely a handful of passengers.

He asked the relief conductor, "Where is everyone? Where are we?"

The new trainman smiled as he replied, "We are west of Bozeman a few miles. That bunch of cowboys got off at Billings, and a couple of families left the train at Columbus – live down Absarokee way. Several people stayed in Bozeman, and only one man got on the train. I understand we're picking up a gang of copper miners in Butte."

"When do I see the mountains? I hear they are grand."

"You could see them if it were daylight. Actually you'll get your fill of the Rockies by the time we reach Spokane. Beautiful scenery but rugged for train travel," the conductor concluded.

Jim nodded and strolled back to his own coach and its hard seat, soon drifting into sleepy reverie, humor bubbling in his thoughts, *My head's about as numb as my behind, but I'm still enjoying my adventure.*

I'm glad I sailed with Captain Kane from Wilmington to New London on that tug and barge. I had a fine visit with Steffi and Harold, saw New York City, and was paid enough for handling explosives to buy my railroad trip to Tacoma. Saying good-bye to the Skipper was hard, and I told him I'd always remember him as my 'guardian uncle.'

I guess my sister was right, Hans always wanted the family farm more than his siblings. When I paid my final visit to Momma, he was barely civil until he heard I was heading for the Klondike. As I look back without malice darkening my thoughts, my brother is the farmer and cares well for his own family, including our mother. Still I made sure Momma and I were alone when I handed her a twenty-dollar gold coin and gave her a final kiss good-bye. I cut all my families ties when I boarded this train headed west.

*****

Bright daylight and the babel of voices combined finally to bring Jim fully awake, aware that he had passed through Butte and was in the Rocky Mountains. He rotated his head gently to loosen his stiff neck, repeating the procedure with his arms, legs and spine. Catching the amused observance of a gray-haired and wrinkled old man seated across the aisle, he grinned in consonance with his neighbor and explained, "Damnable place to catch a bit of sleep. I'll be glad to get to Tacoma."

Winking broadly so his bushy gray brows almost touched his cheek, the old-timer replied, "Know what you mean, young man. My name is Zack Spiros, and I'm headed home for Steilacoom. Time for me to get back to work."

"Oh, aren't you miner? The conductor told me a bunch of miners were boarding this train in Butte. By the way, I'm Jim Gerber from Scranton, Pennsylvania."

Zack acknowledged the introduction with a nod, explaining his slight accent, "I came to this country from Pireaus, Greece as a youngster and fought for the Union in the Civil War. I am an American citizen and have lived in Washington since it became a state ten years ago. I'm a deckhand on the *Talequah*. She's a packet that sails all around the Puget Sound."

Jim listened with interest to the Spiros family history and Zack's job before remarking, "I sailed on riverboats along the Delaware River and on a tugboat up to Long Island Sound. I've been debating whether to strike out on the Klondike gold rush or find a berth in Puget Sound. What do you think?"

"You can talk to my skipper when we get to Tacoma, or to Andrew Foss the tugboat owner. I'm sure we can find you a job. You'd better stay away from the Klondike unless you can afford passage to Skagway and buy a year's supply of grub to carry into Dawson. It sounds good to strike it rich, but only a few prospectors are lucky. Most people I know who went north worked for starvation wages and were glad to be back in Tacoma. It's not for me," Zack concluded then laughingly added an afterthought, "A couple of diehards went back this spring."

The two men discussed the pros and cons of sailing the Puget Sound on packets or tugboats, considered life working steamships to Alaska, and finally talked about salmon fishing in the greater Northwest. Zack shared his sandwich with Jim, along with considerable advice, while Gerber family history and Jim's age raised his new friend's eyebrows.

By the time Spokane was at hand with a bevy of passengers, Zack had slid in beside his young friend to sit, conversation suspended as both tourists studied the "Capital of the Inland Empire" and people-watched for an hour.

*****

Zack awoke from a short nap as their train rumbled over the Columbia River at Wenatchee and picked up his storytelling where he had left off, "Let's see, I told you about Old Man Hill and this railroad, bustling Tacoma or the 'City of Destiny' as it's optimistically labeled, and fishing in the San Juan Islands.

"But Tacoma turned nasty in 1885, at least for the Chinese people in the city. A vigilante committee expelled every Chinaman from the city – railroaded them out of town. Some people hid from the gang but suffered the same fate after they watched their shantytown torched. Some city leaders were involved, so no one was ever prosecuted, and the Chinese still avoid Tacoma. Most Tacomans approve of their Chinese-less city.

"That's almost as wicked a deed as the hanging of Chief Leschi after the Indian War of 1855. Our government was vindictive after they put down the Puget Sound Tribes. Who ever heard of a chief and war leader being hanged for fighting for his land?"

Jim asked in curiosity, "What started the bloodshed?"

"Well, Isaac Stevens came to Washington Territory in 1853 as governor-appointed by President Franklin Pierce. His job was to make peace treaties with all the tribes, which he did zealously whether the Indians wanted a treaty or not. He gathered all the chiefs of Puget Sound tribes at Medicine Creek in the Nisqually Valley not far from Olympia. It was Christmas of fifty-four and he had them sign their X's to a treaty.

Chief Leschi would not give up his Nisqually land rights and refused to sign. When he was summoned to Olympia to answer to Stephens, Leschi refused to go. Before long militia bands and Indian parties were at war, no one knows who fired the first shot. Fighting in the Puget Sound lasted a year or so until regular troops arrived at Fort Steilacoom. Chief Leschi was tried and hung a few months later. Didn't you read about our history in those 'City of Destiny' pamphlets of yours?"

"Not the tales you've told me," Jim replied good-naturedly. "I quit school after the seventh grade to work so I didn't study much history. Say! What's the name of that mountain over there?"

Zack looked ahead and shrugged, "I don't know the

Cascade Mountains from this side, but look at that peak way off to the southwest. It doesn't look like much from here, but it is Mount Tahoma, crown jewel of the south Sound. Folks in Seattle call it Mount Rainier – typical of that bunch. Our two cities argue over most things, a real competition for business leadership. Naturally Olympia, Port Townsend, and Bellingham are ignored by the two 'real' cities of the Puget Sound."

After a brief lull in the conversation, Zach confessed, "My wife and I broke up over the Tacoma-Seattle rivalry. Heh! Heh! She ran off with a Seattle gambling man."

"Does she still live in Seattle?"

"No, she moved to San Francisco years ago. My pride was hurt when she left me, but I'm happy as a bachelor. She said I was a poor husband, and I suspect she was right."

*****

Little conversation was needed after the train passed through Stampede Tunnel and began winding its way down the slopes into the Puget Sound basin. Zach pointed out sights familiar to him, finally muttering in frustration, "Damned rain! Can't even see Tacoma or Seattle with all the clouds. Oh well, we'll be there in an hour."

"I read somewhere it rains here all the time. Is that true?"

Zack laughed caustically, "Ha! Almost true in the winter, but the summer is warm and dry. All that rain keeps our forests green and glorious though."

Jim smiled at the answer, concluding, "We're in for a wonderful summer then, right?"

"Yes, sailing on the *Kalequah* is a pleasure half the year. I'll recommend you to my boss at Puget Sound Freight, and you can enjoy the job as well," Zack paused to change subjects, "Look ahead, that's Tacoma across the Puyallup River."

Jim saw the wide tideflats and bay beyond, city buildings nestling on a hill south and a range of mountains to the west. Zack answered, his raised eyebrow, "Those are the Olympic Mountains beyond Commencement Bay. Look this other way at Gallihan's Gulch, where Tacoma's first sawmill was built in 1854. And the train station is ahead, amidst that bunch of new buildings. Our 'old' Tacoma is west along the shoreline with a score of sawmills cutting lumber. Actually the whole area is your City of Destiny."

"What land is across the bay, beyond that lumber schooner?" Jim queried.

"Vashon and Maury islands with Quartermaster Harbor lying between them are in the middle of the Puget Sound. There are several good beaches for clams, oysters, and geoducks out there. I'll show you a few this summer. Now let's go down to Dock Street. Our train is stopping," Zack said as he gathered his gear and led Jim across the platform to a street heading downhill to the busy waterfront.

Spiros returned a couple of greetings on the street as he opened an office door and ushered Jim inside. A gnome-like Irishman shouted in the squeaky voice of a leprechaun, "Hello Zack! How was your vacation in Montana! You're back a day early. The *Kalequah* comes in tomorrow."

"Howdy, Harry! I figured as much. Had a good time, but I'm ready to sail again. Meet Jim Gerber of Pennsylvania. Worked riverboats and ocean tugboats. He's a fine lad for one of our packets."

The twinkling green eyes set in a wrinkled white face presented a friendly appearance as he said, "I'm Harry Maguire. Any friend of Zack's is welcome at Puget Sound Freight. But how old are you?"

Jim smiled nervously but spoke right up, "I'm eighteen years old this month, and I spent three years on the Delaware River as a boilerman and deckhand and this year as deckhand on a towboat taking Dupont explosives from Wilmington to New London. They even let us pick up a barge of freight in New York City – after we got rid of the powder."

Harry glanced at Spiros again, and after receiving a nod of approval, drew out an employment form, smiling a new kind of welcome, "You're hired, Jim. Five dollars a week, room and board, and one day a week off. Fill in this information for me, and I'll put you in the *Kalequah* today."

Turning to Spiros, Harry asked companionably, "You want to bunk with me tonight, Zack? I'll buy you a beer over at the tavern."

Zack retorted, "Do you think Molly O'Reardon has a fresh coho or silver salmon she'll cook for us?"

Harry slapped the table with open palm, pulling the company form under his eyes as he answered, "Molly always has fresh seafood and a smile for you, Zack."

After another moment he stood erect to shake hands with his new deckhand, welcoming him aboard, "James Kanter Gerber! Jim, your skipper is Captain Roland Trilby. Rollie is uptown this afternoon but will be back sharply at seven o'clock. He lost a sailor to the Klondike gold rush last week in Seattle. He'll be happy to see you. Zack will introduce you to Rollie after he shows you the town."

Jim tactfully ignored his new friend's heighth – or lack of it. Harry's short legs and hunched back brought his eyes up to Jim's chest as the new deckhand responded, "Thank you, Harry. I appreciate the job and I'll be at the *Kalequah* before Captain Trilby returns."

The two sailors left their gear in the office and walked up to Pacific Avenue, Jim gawking at the sights while Zack chattered on. Spiros pointed out several businesses ahead of them, "There's a barbershop, an eatery, a market and an apothecary over there, and across the street is a lumber broker and a bank. Down that…"

"Where's the bank?" Jim interrupted, heading across the street in the direction of a prosperous looking building.

"What's up? I thought you were robbed in Chicago," Zack remarked.

Jim smiled, admitting, "My wallet was stolen, but I have five dollars in gold on me. I'm going to open a savings account in the Bank of Tacoma, and I'm going to add to it every time I'm in town."

*****

Zack and Harry waited with Jim at the packet until Captain Trilby arrived, exchanging greetings and news with the skipper before departing. Rollie was a husky yet gentle Englishman with fair hair and bushy moustache, his hands gnarled and weathered by his profession, yet his face was somehow untouched by the outdoors. He sported a rakish-billed cap similar to many worn by large ship captains, and was invariably clad in a blue jacket with gold braid epaulets. Jim found during the weeks to come Rollie would change to work trousers and boots in rough weather, but never his jacket and cap.

Accompanying the skipper aboard ship Jim found the rest of the crew loafing on the freight deck, no reprimand being given by Rollie. The atmosphere was casual and relaxed although everyone got busy when they sailed. The engineer was a cranky old-timer named William Tell, naturally from Switzerland, who answered to Tellie and nothing else. He was short, wiry, hairless except for a thinning pate, and always greasy. Even though he looked like a dirty bum, there wasn't a man on the Sound who was a better engineer. The only crew member who associated with him was the fourteen-year-old boilerman Tinky, who was homely and not very bright. He reminded Jim of his late brother Gunther, but here there was no affection.

The two deckhands were the brothers Larsen who could pass for twins. Ray was the older and had a tattoo of an anchor on his arm. Roy was the younger and talker with a gold tooth. Ray served as Rollie's unofficial mate and would bare his tattoo when any question of authority arose. Both Larsens wore blue bib overalls and off-white cotton shirts, brown half-boots, and black stocking caps. Each Nordic countenance was fair with blue eyes and fine blond hair.

Jim was accepted by the crew as soon as he handled the lines in casting off. Any man who could do his job was all right with them. Jim was glad to stand quartermaster duties as the *Kalequah* plied the waters of Commencement Bay, and Rollie humored him with names of the twenty odd sawmills on the Old Tacoma shoreline, and then pointed out Ruston Smelter. The Captain took the wheel as they passed Point Defiance and steered the packet into the quiet waters of Gig Harbor for their night moorage.

Chapter 2

Jim scampered up the steep and narrow stairway to the wheel-house after tying the *Kalequah's* line to the town dock. Rollie was closing the windows, and jocularly commented to his new deckhand, "I like a dry cabin, and our June weather is unpredictable. We'll probably see rain before morning."

"I'll remember to secure the wheelhouse, Skipper," Gerber avowed, looking over the rowboat fishing fleet and the sawmills nestled in the snug harbor.

He finally pointed north and queried, "Is that a real Indian camp at the head of the bay?"

"Yes, a few families live up there, mostly Nisqually, Squaxin, and Puyallup. There was a large village on that site just a few years ago, but Gig Harbor fishermen discourage local tribes from staying here. Settlers figure Indians should live in their reservation at Point Fosdick, or their lands on Wollochet Bay," Rollie clarified.

Jim encouraged the captain's dialogue with another question, "Are all of our stops as big as Gig Harbor? By the way, how did it get its name?"

"No, a few stops have a dock, maybe even a store and a few houses, but many times we halt offshore when a settler waves a flag. You'll end up taking men their mail or package in a rowboat while we tread tidal waters. You'll see the Gig Harbor fishing fleet working the Sound from Fox Island to Quartermaster Harbor, although Point Defiance is their favorite fishing ground. Most boats carry eight men, four oars per side, but around here you'll see youngsters in skiffs or canoes.

A lot of these folks are Slovenians or Scandinavians from the old country. The Larsen brothers have kin in Old Tacoma and Ballard as well as Gig Harbor and Steilacoom. Their family moved here when the boys were children.

As to the name, Gig Harbor, a naval captain sent his gig into this cove for exploration and charting in 1841 – a Lieutenant Wilkes as I recall. Early settlers came after the Civil War and liked the colorful title. How about meeting a few townspeople? I'll buy you a beer at the Harbor Inn," Rollie offered.

"Thanks Skipper, one quick beer sounds good. Then I'm off to my bunk. It's been a long day."

*****

The two men left the *Kalequah* in the irascible Telly's hands and walked gingerly along the darkening boardwalk toward the looming shadow of their destination, Rollie leading the way to the doorway of the tavern. Jim stumbled on a loose board just as his comrade muttered a warning, and promptly bumped into the shadowy form of an odoriferous giant of a fisherman. A pair of rough hands shoved him aside as the stranger filled the doorway. Rollie kept Jim upright and waved the newcomer into the lighted room.

"Sorry, mister, my clumsy feet got tangled up," Jim apologized and followed Rollie up the bar.

He climbed aboard a stool next to his boss, and a stein of beer slid along the polished hardwood to stop before him.

"The first one's on Swede, lad. I'm your friendly bartender. Welcome to Gig Harbor," said the craggy-faced old man whose wrinkles gave way to smooth skin just above his full and bushy gray eyebrows. Swede's twinkling blue eyes matched his wide smile as Jim swallowed a mouthful of foam and brew with gusto.

"Good beer, Swede. Thank you. I'm Jim Gerber, Rollie's new deckhand."

"Glad to meet you, Jim. Are you just in from the East Coast?" Swede queried.

Jim laughed as he replied, "My Pennsylvania accent gave me away, right?"

"Ha! Ha! I thought I heard a little New York in your voice, but I was close anyway," Swede teased as he worked the bar.

A heavy hand fell on Jim's shoulder and a deep voice rumbled, "Fellow, you're clumsy and an Easterner to boot. Them's fighting words to Big Einar."

Jim noticed Rollie was watching his reaction with a smile even as he fought down a momentary flash of fear and anger. He'd learned to fight his own battles on the Delaware, but as he looked into the fierce countenance of blond Viking behind him, Jim experienced a serious doubt or two about defending himself. The huge fisherman stood well over six feet tall with broad shoulders, powerful arms and gnarled large hands.

Jim glanced around the suddenly quiet room and spotted the Larsen brothers snickering in glee at a corner table and slowly put two and two together, thinking to himself, *This fellow isn't threatening me. I bet this whole act is a joke on the new deckhand. I wonder who Einar is?*

With the huge paw still clamping his shoulder, Jim looked back at his antagonist and smiled, teasing the burly fisherman in turn, "Well, Einar, you are correct in both instances, but you aren't so big. I have a brother who is bigger and meaner by far. Pull up a stool, and Rollie will buy you a beer."

"Ha! Ha! Ha!" the Viking roared with laughter and then called across the room, "Come over here brothers and buy a round. Your new crew member is young, but he's neither green – nor easily fooled."

Rollie joined the laughing crowd in the barroom, introducing the third Larsen brother to Jim, "Einar, meet Jim Gerber from Pennsylvania. Jim, this hulking galoot is harmless, just as you reckoned. Meet Einar Larsen, another Larsen brother."

*****

Under the morning sun, the crew unloaded cargo consigned to Gig Harbor, Rollie not interested in bucking the outgoing tide. By ten o'clock or so the *Kalequah* cast off lines, eased astern and put her bow into the narrow harbor entrance to cruise Puget Sound. Jim had ample opportunity for sight-seeing as the packet rode the incoming tide between forested cliffs rising three hundred feet on either side of the mile-wide stretch of the Tacoma Narrows.

"Beautiful country, isn't it, Jim?" Rollie asked rhetorically from the open wheelhouse window.

"Yes, sir! It's sure green here in Puget Sound and blue when the sun shines on us."

Rollie nodded as he commented, "All of our rainy weather is great for growing trees and more trees, and sunshine is certainly welcome after last night's showers. Look up ahead, Jim. That bend in the narrows off our starboard bow is Point Evans, and a couple of miles beyond we'll dock at Point Fosdick. We have a lot of cargo to discharge – mostly for the reservation, and we're supposed to pick up a family of five there. I believe they are Fox Island bound – a lonely spot in the summer. Someday we'll stop at the spit to dig a bucket of clams for breakfast. There are a couple of low tides next month while we're in this area."

For an awkward old lady of the inland seas, the *Kalequah* fairly scooted over the smooth surface with the incoming tide, reaching Point Fosdick in but a few minutes. Jim hastened to the boat's lines to secure her to the large dock as Rollie silenced the engine. Only then could the newcomer take a few moments to look over the small crowd gathered on the dock to meet the packet.

"Hey Jim! Catch!" shouted Roy in a mischievous voice. The new deckhand adroitly caught a bolt of dress cloth, and when a spry but pock-marked old Indian woman stepped forward to claim it, he apologized for his partner's antic, "Sorry, ma'am, but no damage done. Are you going to make clothes with this material?"

The woman's face broke into a wrinkled grin, but she didn't answer, an awkward silence broken by a young Indian lad, "Mary's deaf from the pox, mister. She makes good dresses and shirts though."

The deaf lady went her way, and Jim asked curiously, "Do they teach English at your school? You speak it very well, my friend."

"Yes. My name is Harry and I've lived here ever since my father died. I'm a Puyallup and Annie here is a Nisqually. She's pretty new to Point Fosdick," Harry seemed to grow shy after the introductions.

Annie added quietly, "Annie nine, Harry ten. How you?"

Jim replied easily, "I'm Jim Gerber, and I'm eighteen years old. Are you an orphan, too?"

Annie seemed puzzled by his question, Harry quickly explaining, "Yes, she is. Do you have a family, Jim?"

"Only my mother and sister far away, my father died when I was your age. Would you two like to earn a penny apiece?" Jim offered. Roy and Ray sauntered away, leaving the new hand to finish unloading cargo.

People came forward to claim parcels as the trio worked, and soon only a trunk remained on the dock. Rollie called down, "Tote that chest up to the office, Jim. The children can show you the way."

Harry grabbed one leather handle, helping him as Annie hopped ahead of them to the main reservation building. A pair of willing men relieved them of their burden on the covered porch.

Jim handed each youngster a copper coin, smiling inwardly at their sober demeanor in accepting their pay. Annie immediately handed her penny to the lad with a request, "Here Harry. Keep."

Harry nodded as he pocketed the two coins, explaining to

Jim, "Annie is the smallest girl in her class and a newcomer to boot."

Annie smugly inserted, "Harry tough. Nobody steal him."

*****

Jim loaded cargo as the DeLisle family debarked, visiting Lemon Beach near Day Island. A penitentiary official came aboard for the short trip to Steilacoom, and a businessman hitched a ride to Chambers Creek.

Rollie called to Jim, "Take that valise to the McNeil Island boat when we land at Steilacoom. Enjoy our stop but be back within the hour."

Jim grinned a quick response and waved an affirmative signal that he understood. He accompanied their passenger ashore a half-hour later, soon wandering up the streets of the first town of Washington Territory. He watched the open trolley climb the hill toward Tacoma, passengers walking beside their car so the train could manage the grade. It was primitive but effective in carrying people across the county, and he chuckled when an old-timer sitting on a bench nearby joked, "Never could understand why people pay good money to walk up that hill."

After passing the time of day with one of the town's early settlers (and an important citizen in the original county seat, according to the talkative man), Jim entered Bair Drug and Hardware for a sarsaparilla before meandering back to the *Kalequah*.

Roy was full of news, reporting, "We're spending the night at Wollochet Bay, and Rollie says my brother and I can dig clams on the sand spit on Fox Island in the morning. You can handle the freight, can't you?"

The three men moved their cargo around the deck to simplify Jim's job while the Larsens were gone, the new sailor amused at their eagerness to dig clams. He thought it was a lot of work for a clambake.

As they headed north to Fox Island, the *Kalequah* rode the outgoing tide to a stop on the southwest shore and then went around the east end of the island and ran into the strong flow of tidal waters as they struggled past Point Fosdick.

The Skipper smiled at his new hand's look of consternation as they almost came to stop. He explained, "There's no point in

fighting the tide, Jim, we'll just ease along Hale Passage until the
tide changes in an hour or so. Plenty of time to reach Wollochet
Bay and deliver our cargo. It's a fine anchorage for overnight, and
the Larsens will row over to the sand spit and dig clams at low tide
in the morning. They'll have a feast ready for us when we pick
them up in the morning. Have you ever tasted freshly steamed
clams?"

"Yes, once on a trip to lower Delaware Bay. I'm looking
forward to trying Puget Sound clams. I hear geoducks are a local
treat, Rollie," Jim replied.

*****

The *Kalequah* sailed up the eastern shore of Henderson Bay
during the early afternoon, stopping at an array of flagstones and
docks. Jim's memory of names became fuzzy with such places as
Arletta, Horsehead Bay, Raft Island, Rosedale, Purdy and Burley
Lagoon.

Following the sun's shadow into Springfield, or was it
Wuana, Elgin, and Home, the boat traversed the west side of the
bay, finally arriving at Long Branch near twilight for an overnight
anchorage.

*****

Jim awoke before dawn the next morning to the sound of
raindrops striking the *Kalequah*, jumping to the deck and dressing
in haste before running to the wheelhouse. He found Rollie closing windows and standing in a puddle of rainwater, grinning self-
effacedly as he greeted his deckhand, "Argh! I forgot my own rule,
Jim. Never expected it to rain. You'd better go below and help the
Larsen brothers come aboard. I see their friend is rowing them
alongside."

"Yes, sir!" Jim complied quickly as he skipped stairs to
reach the cargo deck and assist his shipmates.

Arguing voices carried through the damp night air, Jim able
to make out the brothers slurred words to confirm their intoxicated
state. He thought, *They were drunk last night when I left them for
my bunk.*

Slipping on the wet steel grating by the cargo door, Jim
yelled a warning, "Careful mates! The deck is wet."

He reached forward to grasp Ray's hand in a firm grip and wrestle him aboard, both hands and patience needed as he propelled the older brother to dry decking. A drunken curse from Roy turned into a muffled scream and loud splash as the sailor slipped into the water between the rowboat and the *Kalequah*. Their friend sat aghast at his oar, movement frozen as he yelled, "I can't swim. Where is Roy?"

Jim jumped feet first into the void between vessels, sinking a dozen feet below the surface in search of his shipmate, and by pure happenstance felt a shirttail fluttering in his fingertips. He closed his fist around the material and pulled his struggling friend's head out of the water, Rollie grabbing Roy's shirt collar, dragged his torso up the side onto the deck.

Roy leaned over the side, coughed and regurgitated his stomach's contents over Jim, who hastily ducked below the surface to scrub himself clean. The young man was not in a good mood when he bobbed back to fresh air. In fact he grumpily insisted on crawling aboard the deck by himself, not wanting either Larsen's assistance. He headed for the shower and a dry set of work clothes, saying nary a word to anyone.

*****

The morning sum broke through patchy clouds to warm Jim as he accomplished morning chores alone. The Larsen brothers' snoring was part of the background noise as the *Kalequah* sailed around Devil's Head into Carr Inlet. He learned another round of names and places as the packet made a half-dozen stops on the eastern shore.

As they crossed the head of the waterway, Rollie called out of an open window, "Next stop is Allyn, Jim. We are now in Mason County and are headed down the west side of Harstine Island to the Squaxin Indian Reservation. Maybe we can spend the night in Shelton. Are you holding up all right?"

"Sure, Skipper, let Ray and Roy sleep off their binge. Maybe I can loaf some tomorrow. When do we get to Olympia?" Jim queried.

Rollie laughed in agreement, "Yes, they can handle our flag stops down to Olympia. Would you be willing to take Tinky to visit his grandmother. She's his only living kin, and he gets scared in crowded places."

Jim nodded, not looking forward to the task but willing, "Yes, I'll help as long as Tinky will show me the state capital before we return to the *Kalequah*."

*****

"Don't forget to take some flowers to your Grandma, Tinky," was the engineer's quiet instruction to his young helper. The lad was silent as he walked dutifully beside Jim up the board-walk toward downtown Olympia.

Recalling his youth on the farm when his brother Gunther was his playmate, Jim began a casual but one-sided conversation with Tinky. He talked about Seattle and Tacoma without much more than a polite yes or no from the lad, but when he began recounting their voyage from Shelton earlier in the day, Tinky corrected him about Harstine and Hope Islands, reminding Jim that Boston Harbor had been their last flag stop before docking in Olympia.

"This is Budd Inlet, Jim. Mud Bay is over there. The Captain doesn't go in there. It's pretty shallow. Oh gosh! There's Wally, he always picks on me. Calls me a 'Dummy'."

Jim put a hand on the agitated boy's shoulder, ignoring the bully as he offered, "I like lemon drops. Can we buy some in this store? I see some tulips for sale, too. Maybe your grandmother would like a few flowers."

Tinky nodded nervously in agreement, hurrying to the back counter of the general store to peer into the candy case. Jim watched him select lemon drops and licorice sticks, and stepped forward to pay, "This is my treat, Tinky. You buy the flowers."

The storekeeper called the boy by name when he asked, "Well, Tinky, what would you like?"

"How much for six tulips, Mister Morris?"

"Eight cents, young fellow. They cost fifteen cents a dozen," the man explained carefully.

"Then I'll take a dozen," Tinky responded thoughtfully, looking to Jim for approval before handing Mister Morris a nickel and a dime. The storekeeper's face wore a surprised smile as he completed the transaction and spoke a gentle farewell, "Thank you, Tinky," with a tone of respect the lad appreciated by grinning happily.

"Hey Dummy! You bothering folks around here again? I'll take those flowers, thank you," the bully accosted a cringing Tinky.

"No...for...Grandma," stuttered the frightened boy. "You're Dummy, and I'll take them if I want."

Jim sidled between the boys, taking the tulips in hand as he moved aside, noticing the cocky lad was neither larger nor more muscular than his shipmate. Gerber the peacemaker said, "Maybe we should go to your grandmother's now."

A larger edition of Wally, no doubt his brother, laughed raucously in a challenging manner, "Go ahead and poke Dummy in the nose. His friend is a scared dummy, too."

Without conscious thought Jim moved a step right and swung the back of his hand across the older bully's face, a large welt raising under his eye even as the boys stood aghast.

Jim felt a blow from behind and turned sideways to Tinky pulling Wally back by his ears. The spluttering older brother stepped forward to intercede, and Jim kicked his legs out from under him, backing the scrambling figure into the dust-filled gutter. Without a word from Jim, Tinky spun Wally about and tripped him atop his brother in the street.

The two yahoos crawled out of reach, cursing their conquerors as they ran away. Jim said simply, "Thanks, Partner! Here's your flowers, let's go see grandma. I want you to show me the Capitol building later."

*****

Jim was nibbling on cheese and crackers in the galley late that evening, somewhat startled as he looked up to find the greasy old engineer standing in the doorway, Tinky almost hidden in the shadows beyond. Unsure of Tellie's expression, Jim pushed his simple fare across the cold stone with a friendly offer, "Have a bite, Tellie. I couldn't sleep until I put something in my stomach. You too, Tinky. Are you hungry?"

"Thanks, don't mind if I do," Tellie accepted a dainty bite or two while scrutinizing Gerber, finally drawing a greasy pint bottle from his hip pocket and proffering it to his shipmate with a cackle.

As Jim sipped a swallow of moonshine, Tellie grinned widely and cackled anew, "Wish I'd been there, Jim. Did my boy Tinky really whip that Wally? He's usually too easy-going."

Aware of the lad's presence, Jim phrased his response carefully, "Your helper was determined to follow your orders and take flowers to his grandma. Even then he didn't throw that bully into the street until we had a good fight brewing. He's growing into a fine young man, Tellie. You're training him well."

At a loss for words ,all the old-timer could say was, "Have another drink, Jim. Tinky get in here. Damned if you don't deserve a drink, too."

Rollie appeared behind the lad with a booming voice declaring, "I don't know about that, mates. An Olympia police officer told me that my crew beat up the sheriff's nephews. Ha! Ha! I wish I had been there. Give me a slug, Tellie, and then we'd better move this boat away from the dock in case that paragon of local law comes looking for us."

Rollie hiccupped as the potent brew went down his gullet, but laughed easily at the situation. Tinky was a man today, even the Larson brothers agreeing as they heard the story and moved the *Kalequah* offshore.

*****

Jim enjoyed standing the quartermaster watch as the packet left Nisqually Reach and Anderson Island behind them, riding the outgoing tide to Tacoma. The Skipper never said a word as he observed his new deckhand with a pleased expression. His opinion was reaffirmed – Gerber was young in age but wealthy in sailing experience.

Cruising around the majestic bluff of Point Defiance, Jim realized the tide was turning and quickly rang the engine room for more power. Tellie was aware the youngster was at the wheel and responded with alacrity.

"Well I swear! Our ornery shipmate likes you. Taking care of Tinky earned you a place of respect with the engineer. Good work, Jim. Now let's head for home."

*****

Later that evening Jim was munching on a stale sandwich when Harry rapped on the open cabin door, asking companionably, "Are you interested in sharing a bucket of beer with me before I go home? I have some crackers and cheese, too."

"You bet, Harry, and thanks," the lad responded forthwith. "Rollie said it was all right to sleep aboard, and Tinky gave me his lunch – from yesterday I bet. Beer and cheese sound wonderful to me."

Offering his friend the only stool in the crew's quarters, Jim found two tin cups and sat opposite Harry on his bunk. A philosophical discussion ensued, garnering considerable polish as the beer bucket ran dry.

*****

Awakening to the bumbling sounds of a hungover Harry as he staggered from Tinky's bunk outside to the nearest rail, Jim sighed half aloud, "Harry, don't fall overboard."

He rolled out to stand on bare feet and follow his new friend. Harry was leaning over the side but clinging firmly to the wooden bar, and Jim smiled gently as he turned toward his warm bunk. A splashing sound reverberated importunately over the city waterway and its still damp air. He shook his head in wonder as he saw Harry frozen in place, the clerk suddenly gurgling an ambiguous alarm, "What's that? A man overboard? Yes…a man in the water out there…Jim, I can't swim. Help!"

Barefoot or not, Jim moved swiftly across the deck to pause momentarily beside Harry, his eyes following the clerk's pointing finger to the shadowed surface near their bow where waterfront lamps cast a phosphorescent gleam over the ripple in the water.

Jim shouted loudly, "Man overboard! Forward of the *Kalequah*!," and added in calming tones to Harry, "Throw a couple of life rings after me."

Jim leaped away from the packet's side, landing feet first in the cold water and submerging into the cold and clammy depths before finally bobbing to the surface. He struck out for a nightlight on the next vessel forward of the packet, Harry's first ring toss almost scoring a point as water splashed in his face. A second cork float landed just a few feet away as Harry called out, "Straight on, Jim. I'll go for help."

Pushing two life rings ahead of him, Jim began treading water as he blinked the briny drops from his blurry eyes. His heart jumped in shock as a subterranean monster crawled up his left leg, the bewildered sailor realizing somewhat belatedly that a groping hand had grabbed him. He grasped the extended fingers and pulled them through one cork lifesaver, followed moments later by a sputtering head.

As both swimmers managed to drape arms over the floats and drift safely on the bay's surface, Jim asked, "Are you all right, fellow?"

"Cough...yes thanks...now that I'm frozen sober. So much for a night on the town with my college buddies," retorted the rough voice of a young man. As an afterthought he added, "Two hoodlums robbed me of my coins and pocket watch. Hmm! Why did they throw me in bay?"

A call from shore rang out, "Hello, Jim! Where are you? Let out a yell, and we'll throw you a line."

Both swimmers responded with a spate of noise, and a rope slapped water between them. Their rescue was imminent.

*****

Howard Anderson straightened his shoulders, steadied his gait and faced the filigree-glassed front door of his family home near Wright Park. He took a deep breath before announcing, "I can walk into my house, Jim. You go on back to your boat – and thanks!"

Jim glanced at his unsteady friend and then the opening door, which soon framed a frowning and disapproving older woman – Howard's mother as revealed by the still tipsy college graduate, "Hello Momma, I...er...I've been at a party."

"And drinking I see and smell!" scolded Missus Anderson, gently turning to lambaste Howard's companion, "I suppose you're the cause of my son's intemperance, you rascal you. Can't you miscreants leave poor Howard alone. You ought to be ashamed of yourself, leading him astray with such debauchery. Be gone, you scoundrel, and never darken my doorstep again."

"Mother, Jim never...", Howard's objection was waved away imperiously by the red-faced mother, still glaring angrily at the sailor.

Jim nodded and agreed, "Yes, ma'am. Good night, Howard," and hastily withdrew in discomfort, thoroughly cowed by the woman's wrath. He thought, *Golly, I'm innocent of any wrongdoing, might even be a hero, but I'll never convince Missus Anderson of anything.*

His laughter was barely checked as he caught a second look of disdain from a girl in the window, Howard's sister shaking her finger at him in reproof. He strode into the vacant street, seeing the humor in his chastisement and laughed merrily to himself. No use getting Howard into more trouble was his irreverent notion.

He found his warm bunk on the packet without any delay.

This afternoon they would sail to Dockton on Maury Island before proceeding to Gig Harbor. He was happy in his new job and summer in Puget Sound, even Howard's dilemma was a refreshing adventure.

Chapter 3

The first major storm of the fall was raging across the Puget Sound, with the *Kalequah* battened up and running before the wind off Point Evans. Jim followed the Skipper's orders automatically, moving the wheel a point starboard or port as southwesterly gusts pushed the packet askew and a strong incoming tide impeded her progress. Washington rain pummeled the roof and windows of the wheelhouse in the dim visibility of the Tacoma Narrows.

Rollie quipped, "Who would think it's noon in this dismal light? Tinky likes the simple joke that it's 'Oregon mist' – the rain missed Oregon and hit us. Well Jim, get used to it. We'll see this weather all winter athough it's better than fog or snow for sailing. We'll reach our berth in Tacoma before dark anyway, probably a half-hour after the tide turns."

"So the rainy season is here, Captain. I did enjoy our lovely summer," Jim replied with a grimace.

"Yeah, we earn our wages for a few months now. Almost feel guilty about collecting any pay during the summer," Rollie sallied as he wiped the windows with a clean rag.

Jim's thoughts drifted into a pleasant reverie, memories stirring his uncounscious images of the past summer. *I'll take my pay thank you. I deposited most of it in the Bank of Tacoma, new clothes an exception when Missus Anderson personally invited me to supper last month. It seems Howard explained I was a good guy.*

Ha! Ha! I missed a home-cooked meal when Howard accepted a position at the reservation school at Point Fosdick. This morning my new friend reinvited me to stay with the Andersons over the Christmas holidays – three days anyway. The Kalequah is in port that long.

I'll have to save some time for Tellie's party. He's downright pleasant these days since his protégé Tinky punched Wally in the nose again last trip. The lad has found his backbone as well as put on twenty poinds of muscle this past summer. The bully will leave him alone after that ruckus. Maybe I can talk Tellie into celebrating the Christmas holiday in that same Olympic Hotel where Tinky vanquished his bully foe.

*****
The *Kalequah* slipped into its berth on the city waterway in the early morning hours of the day before Christmas, the Skipper keeping his promise to the crew for a three-day holiday. Howard Anderson and the South Sound mail were the only cargo on the last leg of their voyage.

As soon as Jim finished his chores and changed clothes, the two friends sauntered across Pacific Avenue. Howard suggested, "Let's shop our way home. Did you get paid?"

"Yes, Harry came aboard while you were getting your bag. I thought I'd buy your mother a shawl and your sister a pin. Is that a good idea?" Jim asked tentatively, not having much recent experience with buying Christmas gifts.

"Sure! And I can use a new tie for my classroom outfit. Ha! Ha! Are you buying for anyone else?"

Jim wagged his head in a negative response, "No, our crew traded gifts at Tinky's party in Olympia, and Rollie is buying Harry our gift today – spirits, of course. I did send my mother a photograph of the *Kalequah* last week. I'm not very close to my family as you can see."

Jim enjoyed the walk across town, shopping with zest if not spending much money. Howard was a spender by nature and was carrying three bags of presents up Saint Helens Avenue when Jim came to an abrupt halt before a small jewelry store tucked between a smoke shop and a bakery.

Gazing fixedly into the window, he murmured half to himself, "I bought a locket and chain just like that for my sister Steffi this spring. Would your sister like it?" Jim asked eagerly, a hint of seasonal nostalgia aquiver in his voice.

"Well yes, of course, but didn't you buy her a cameo brooch back there on Pacific?" Howard queried with concern, adding, "Can you afford it?"

"Let's go see, Howard," Jim replied happily as he entered the store and haggled over prices with the elderly gentleman proprietor. Offering a swap of the brooch and a handful of coins, he walked away with a prettily wrapped small package which he immediately sealed in the pocket of his peajacket.

"Ha! Ha! I reckon you're broke now, eh?" Howard tendered with jovial humor.

Jim dug deep into his other pocket and produced a silver

dollar, grinning at his good fortune as he turned into the bakery. He purchased a box of mixed Christmas cookies and talked the proprietor into selling him a bunch of asters displayed behind the counter. Howard ended up paying for them as his friend's last dollar went over the counter.

*****

Hurrying up the street to the familiar front door and following closely on Howard's heels through it and upstairs, the two young men sighed in unison. They had reached Howard's bedroom without disclosing their bundles' contents as they dumped them on his bed behind the closed door.

Women's voices called from the foot of the staircase, Jim shaking his head as his friend was deaf to the calls, observing, "Maybe you can ignore your mother, but I can't."

Whereupon he gathered the bouquet of flowers and left his laughing host to descend the stairs and offer the blossoms to Missus. Anderson.

"Oh how nice, James. Thank you. But where is my wayward son?"

"Taking care of our gift purchases, ma'am. He'll be down in a few minutes. I want to thank you for inviting me to your home for Christmas. It's been years since I had a real Christmas celebration," Jim admitted with chagrin.

"Oh my, and you're only eighteen years of age. Did you leave home as a boy?" Missus Anderson quizzed her guest with a confused look.

"Mother told me I had to mind my big brother, but I chose not to. She lives with Hans' family on the Gerber farm near Scranton. At least my nasty temper and stubborn nature saved me from being a farmer."

"Do you have any other brothers or sisters?" his curious hostess continued.

"Just my little sister Steffi and her family in Connecticut. My other two brothers are dead. What about you, Missus Anderson? I know Howard has a sister named Esther. Didn't I hear her voice earlier? Do you have family in Tacoma?"

"Just my late husband's bachelor brother Carl in Old Tacoma. His fishing boat is beached there. My poor husband fell off Carl's boat in Alaska and drowned two summers ago. My brother-in-law will come for dinner tomorrow. What is that racket I hear upstairs? Esther, are you peeking at your brother's gifts? Come down here and meet his friend," Missus Anderson concluded with a grin and a shrug.

Jim had been studying Howard's mother as they chatted, admiring both the matriarch and the lady in her persona. Mary Anderson somehow appeared younger than his own mother even though both of them must be near the same age. The Gerber son thought in retrospect, *Momma's long gray hair and wrinkles make her seem older than forty-eight years. Missus Anderson's hair is short, curly, and brunette. Because of a fancy beauty parlor? She looks too young to be Howard's mother. I betcha that...*

"Jim, meet my daughter Esther. Dear, our guest is James Gerber," Mary Anderson stated and interrupted his semi-reverie.

Turning his gaze to meet the entrancing green eyes of a pretty young lady, Jim was doubly tongue-tied by his wool-gathering and her charm. He wasn't acquainted with young ladies nor was he socially adept. Feeling like a clod, he barely managed "Hello!"

Esther's eyes twinkled with either amusement of conquest – or both. Jim couldn't tell which but breathed a sigh of relief when Howard joined his family and distracted attention from his callow behavior. His friend had told him that Esther was fifteen years old, but she sure seemed older than Jim felt at that moment.

"Jim, come help me wrap gifts before my kid sister sneaks in my room again. Mom, when's supper?"

"In an hour or so, Son. Olympia oysters, right? Ha! Ha! And a bottle of beer for you young men."

*****

The Northwest supper culminated with Christmas pudding, with Jim unabashedly eating his second helping as the voices of a wandering choir echoed through the damp air of Wright Park. Esther ran to the front window, spreading the curtains in excitement as she cried, "Howard, our neighborhood friends are caroling outside. Let's go join them. Jim, can you carry a tune?"

Shaking his head with a rueful smile, he replied, "Not in a bucket, Esther. You two go ahead, and I'll walk your mother over to the Community Church on Tacoma Avenue."

"Oh, I forgot. Mother, I'm sorry," the girl bemoaned, even as she looked hopefully across the room.

"That's all right Dear, you go ahead with Howard. He'll watch after you and bring you home early, right Son?"

With a pair of nods, brother and sister darted out the door, dressing warmly as they raced after the impromptu carol group.

Without a word Jim began clearing the supper table, china, silver and serving dishes reaching the kitchen sink in no time. He earned a warm smile of appreciation from Mary as she joshed him, "Tell me about your mother, someone must have taught you good manners. I wish my children were as thoughtful."

"Ha! Ha! I can't remember volunteering very often at home, but your cooking deserves my applause – and help. What time is your church service?"

*****

Jim was lying abed when Howard slipped into his room quietly, not wanting to disturb his guest. "How was caroling, Howard?" Jim asked softly, his friend quick to offer a reply.

"Great! You should have come along. A neighbor treated everyone to hot cider and ginger snaps. Say, thanks for keeping Momma company. I'm not much of a church-goer, just a family escort for Momma and Esther," Howard admitted.

"Me, too," Jim concurred, "but I enjoyed visiting with Mary. She's sure smart. I felt like an ignoramus talking to her. You know, I quit school too young to be a good conversationalist."

"Conversationalist, eh?" Howard chuckled and suggested, "That's a big word. You're pretty sharp yourself, and it's never too late to go to school. Now go to sleep, we open gifts at first light in this house."

*****

Opening more than one gift was a rarity for Jim on any Christmas, and now he had four presents before him. Uncle Carl had joined the household before anyone was fully awake, bringing packages of smoked salmon and a bottle of schnapps for after dinner. Hot chocolate and toast with blackberry jam greeted the holiday revelers as they opened their gifts, Esther shrieking with joy when she opened Jim's gift to her.

Sidling over to the young man, she asked, "It's beautiful, Jim. Thank you. Will you put it around my neck?"

Jim flushed as his clumsy fingers brushed her creamy soft skin at her neck, sure he was happier with giving more than she appreciated the receiving. Words of romantic action crossed his mind but never reached his lips as he was unable to ask her to go walking later in the day.

Moments later as the gift exchange came to a satisfying conclusion, Esther deflated Jim's euphoria. There was a knock on the door, and the girl announced, "Oh, that must be Edgar. We're going walking in the park."

Mary frowned at her daughter, issuing a mild rebuke, "Why haven't I heard of your plans, Esther? Uncle Carl and Jim are our guests today."

"Oh Momma, I'll be back in time to help with dinner, and Howard and I will give Jim a tour of Wright Park and our fancy Northern Pacific Hotel tomorrow."

Jim forced a smile to his lips as he waved good-bye to Esther, depression settling over his cheerful Yuletide feelings. He spent the morning playing matchstick poker with Carl and Howard, Mary joining them when she put the goose in the oven. Uncle Carl was elated when the game ended with all the matchsticks piled in front of him, Howard laughing as he teased the old fisherman, "You won all the money – must be all of fifteen cents in front of you. Ha! Ha!"

They were exchanging jibes when Esther returned with her Edgar, having invited him to Christmas dinner. The mother smiled concurrence as she set another place at the table, then another rap sounded at the door.

Howard answered the knock, opening the door with a cheerful "Merry Christmas!" and Jim recognized Tinky's voice raised in a hesitant reply.

"Who is it, Howard?" his mother called, stepping forward to meet their awkward and flustered visitor.

Howard answered gently, "Jim's shipmate Tinky has come with a message for him."

The lad stepped forward with hat in hand, clean and neat in his best work clothes, stuttering nervously, "We have to sail tonight Jim."

Jim heard a snickered aside from Edgar, which produced a tinkled laugh from Esther, a flash of anger clouding Jim's eyes. He hadn't liked Edgar much anyway, but his real anger was directed at Esther for being so insensitive.

"Merry Christmas, Tinky. I'm glad to see you. Let me introduce Howard's family. This lady is his mother, Mary Anderson, and Carl Anderson is his uncle and a fishing boat captain. His sister Esther and her friend Edgar are just back from a walk in Wright Park. Folks meet my friend Theodore Tinker of Olympia. His Grandma calls him Theodore but his friends call him Tinky," Jim concluded his staccato introduction with a sharp glance to silence Edgar's second snicker.

Mary's knowing glance followed Jim's, Esther turning sober as Edgar openly sneered at their visitor. She turned to the lad and offered, "I hope you can join us for dinner, Theodore. Any friend of Jim's is a friend of ours."

The boy nodded happily, mouth agape as he sought Jim's approval before accepting, "Yes, ma'am. Thank you, ma'am," turning to Jim to explain. "Captain says we're going to Poulsbo at five o'clock. The *Kalequah* is on the beach, and her captain is hurt...oh...Zack is fine."

Jim breathed a sigh of relief at the news of his friend, ignoring Edgar's continual boorish behavior. Carl quickly stepped into the hiatus in conversation and told an interesting tale of Ketchikan and its famous King Salmon. Jim said little during the meal, Howard and his mother injecting holiday sentiments into the gloomy atmosphere.

*****

Howard and his mother walked the two sailors to their front door at dark, Carl waving a casual good-bye as they left the house among "Thanks" and "Happy New Year." Esther and Edgar were silent in the parlor, and Jim shrugged away a negligible sigh of remorse as they walked down the street. His companion had been silent at dinner but was voluble in his praise of Missus Anderson and his wonderful day with her family.

When Tellie met them at the gangplank, the lad continued his elated jabbering, Jim smiling as he winked at the engineer. Captain Trilby chuckled as he queried, "Well, he is sure hungry, isn't he?"

"Our shipmate had 'Christmas dinner' with the Anderson family, and Mary Anderson called him a young gentleman," Jim explained.

Rollie nodded thoughtfully before suggesting, "Maybe we need to buy Tinky a set of nice clothes if he's going social on us. I'll suggest it to Tellie."

"Hey, Skipper, are we loaded? Where are we headed? When do we sail?" called Ray from the dock as the two brothers appeared at the gangway.

Rollie answered promptly, "Yes, let loose the lines. Jim, you can change clothes after we clear the city waterway. For now our heading is Brown's Point. Watch for two lumber schooners anchored off Old Tacoma. We have some rough weather for our voyage to Poulsbo."

*****

It was raining cats and dogs along the Kitsap shoreline as they maneuvered alongside the hapless *Talequah*, pumps working loudly as she lay at anchor thirty feet from Poulsbo's town pier. The white caps of Puget Sound were absent in the snug harbor, and both crews were able to transfer over the ton of cargo in an hour's time.

Jim found a moment to seek out Zack Spiros in the *Talequah's* wheelhouse. He stated formally, "Permission to come aboard, Captain," his teasing grin softening the joke.

"Hah! Some captain I'd be. I was at the wheel when the Skipper slipped and fell down the stairs. He was discombobulated by a rap on his head for a few moments before anyone let me know. Why, I barely had time to reverse engines before bottoming out this 'Old Lady'. High tide let me float her free, but we have a leak. It's off to the Duwamish boatyard for repairs in the morning."

Jim guffawed in consolation, "Yah, my friend. I heard the *Kalequah* would have sunk if you hadn't saved her – a real hero – and her acting captain."

"Ha! Ha!" both men laughed at what had been a dire situation as Jim stated, "Just another day on Puget Sound, eh Captain?" The two chatted for several minutes until Rollie called for his quartermaster.

As soon as he stepped up to the wheel, the Skipper ordered, "Lines away!" and then instructed Jim, "Bring her slowly to starboard and set a course between those two lights to the south. Let's stay in the middle of the channel tonight. And speak up if you see any other vessel. We'll slip through the passage between the peninsula and Bainbridge Island. Zack asked us to deliver a package to Suquamish. You know, where Chief Seattle is buried."

Jim nodded as he peered into the darkness ahead, finally asking, "Port Townsend or Whidby Island?"

"Yes, in that order, Jim. Then Ebey's Landing and south around Whidby for several stops until we reach La Conner. Oh yes, another package is destined for Hope Island in Skagit Bay. We have four days to get back to Tacoma and make our South Sound schedule. Not much chance for any time off until the middle of January – next century. Ha! Ha!"

*****

Whitecaps sprayed the cumbersome packet, the shallow-drafted vessel, rolling precariously off-center keel as they left Port Townsend. Rollie immediately ordered Ray to run southerly, skipping the stop at Ebey's Landing and ignoring two flags along the western shore of Whidby Island. Everyone on the crew breathed a sigh of relief when they reached Clinton at dusk, laying over to discharge cargo in the morning.

Jim felt the boat rocking heavily before dawn, wakening to a change in wind direction which caused Rollie to unload cargo by lamplight. Even then the fenders were banging against the dock all the while.

Jim left the village store last and turned to accept the signed receipt from the storekeeper. Ray and Roy untied the gangplank in preparation to heave it aboard when the *Kalequah* shook violently and jarred the gangplank loose. Jim stepped to the end of the dock as salty spray drenched his face and body, the young sailor reaching forward to steady himself with the gangplank railing even as it dropped to the turbulent water below.

Blinking his eyes to clear his vision, Jim saw the dilemma he faced as he leaned off balance and tried to stop. A gust of wind nudged his backside as he teetered on the brink of catastrophe, and in seeming slow motion he toppled into the Puget Sound.

A call of "Man overboard!" sounded as he entered the water headfirst, the chilly temperature sparking an immediate reaction from the hapless swimmer. An initial thought to get out of the bay was followed by the bright side of his misfortune, he hadn't hit the gangplank. He surfaced between the packet and the pilings, diving to clear the danger of being crushed and swimming in the direction of shore.

A resonant thud struck his ears before he surfaced again, finding his fortune was good as the boat slammed into the dock once more. Jim struggled to the rocky shore, spitting out seawater as he came erect in the icy wind. A small group of Clinton residents surrounded the shivering survivor, Roy running forward with a blanket and a relieved yet laughing remark, "Just another day of work, eh Jim?"

*****

Dry clothes, hot soup and an hour's rest in the warm galley was just what Jim needed before returning to duty at Langley. Rollie assigned him as quartermaster so he kept decently dry and comfortable, stopping at Greenbank, Coupeville, Oak Harbor and Hope Island. He helped the Larsens unload cargo at La Conner, the prospect of a hot meal and calm waters making the *Kalequah's* overnight stay almost enjoyable.

Rollie escorted five passengers aboard in the morning, the Helmsen family bound for Winslow on Bainbridge Island where Sven was a well-known storekeeper and his son Harold was his partner. Howard the grandson was eight years old and full of questions while granddaughter Sharon was fourteen years old and quiet. Jim was given the task of keeping the family safe inside the galley or the crew's quarters.

Howard was an active handful to manage by midafternoon, when he finally succumbed to his energetic adventure by falling asleep on Jim's bunk. Sharon proved to be bright and cheerful company who chatted about her uncle and aunt and cousins in La Conner as well as her school days at Winslow. It was obvious to Jim that he was lacking education, a conclusion he'd figured out during Christmas dinner with the Andersons. Jim talked easily with the girl because she was obviously impressed with the older young man who was a real sailor.

Missus Helmsen looked peaked, and Sharon informed Jim that she was queasy with pregnancy and seasick to boot. He made up the spare bunk and so that Abigail could rest, asked the girl, "You want to help in the galley? I've got to warm up a pot of stew and pan fry some bread. Everyone will be hungry before we reach your home."

"Ha! Ha! Not Momma. Yes, I'm a good cook – and hungry already," Sharon responded with a warm smile, happy to be included in his job.

An hour later they carried bowls of stew to the men in the wheelhouse and then served themselves and a groggy Howard in the crews' cabin. Abigail even asked for a portion as they plied the calmer waters approaching Winslow.

*****

The *Kalequah* nudged into her pier on the city waterway after midnight, Harry Maguire coming aboard with sailing orders. Everyone worked all night loading cargo and supplies, Harry returning at dawn with mail, special delivery packages and pay envelopes. His teasing fell on deaf ears, Jim for one too tired to react. All was forgiven however when their wages included two extra dollars, one coin for Christmas and the other for missing a day off. By eight o'clock the packet was underway, bound for Gig Harbor and manned by six groggy sailors.

Chapter 4

Jim Gerber stood at ease to one side of the wheelhouse as the Skipper wended through the flotsam released by a high tide, heading down the Narrows on the way home. The young sailor's mind wandered deep in thought over his visit last evening with Howard Anderson, Puyallup Harry, Nisqually Annie and three other bright pupils at Point Fosdick School. *Boy, was I dumb. I mean, I didn't say a word because they all knew answers before I could read the questions. I wonder if Tacoma High School has any about-to-be nineteen year old students. Ha! As if I belonged in a real high school.*

Gee, I felt just like I did last week when I visited with the Helmsens in Gig Harbor. Sharon likes me, and her girl friend flirted with me, but her folks frowned at me a lot. Probably think I'm not good enough for their daughter – and they're right. Ah well, they went back to Winslow in their fancy sailboat.

I wonder if I'd be as smart as Edgar if I were in school. He's a yahoo, fancy words and manners or not. Esther ignored me when I delivered a package from Howard at Easter, but Mary fed me a scrumptious ham supper at least. This shipboard life is kind of boring. Oh well, I ...

"What's up, Jim? You seem a little blue this morning," the captain inquired in a solicitous manner.

"Just daydreaming, Rollie. Why is it the girls I know are all smarter than me? I wish I had gone to school longer."

His friend kept his silence, realizing the question was rhetorical. Jim would have to solve that problem his own way. Rollie suspected that he'd lose a deckhand when he figured it out. With that thought he turned the wheel over to the young sailor and did some daydreaming of his own.

*****

Two celebrations of his nineteenth birthday caused mixed feelings for Jim, his actual birthdate falling on a day the *Kalequah* was Point Fosdick. Harry, Annie and three other Indian students threw a Nisqually potlatch for the sailor and his friends from the packet. Jim was pleased at all the attention and proud to be a "South Sounder."

On his return to Tacoma, he had two letters waiting for him with the company clerk Harry, one a card from his mother wishing him a happy birthday – a rare treat for the former Pennsylvanian. The second message was an invitation from the Andersons for a special day supper on his return to port.

He appreciated the gesture and was enjoying the conversation and gift opening when Esther brought her beau Edgar home for the informal meal. The Tacoma High School graduate was just as conceited as ever, and his feigned friendliness toward Jim covered an officious attitude of superiority which got on the sailor's nerves. Esther's silly giggling was irritating to Jim, but everyone else ignored it.

Jim and Howard contrived to leave early and frequent a tavern on Pacific Avenue, erasing the lad's dour outlook on his day. His friend's advice given sober first and tipsy later was, "Don't let Edgar get on your nerves, Jim-buddy. So Old Man Randall is a banker, his son hasn't worked a day in his life. He enrolled in the University of Washington because he's jealous of your adventures – and your maturity. Ignore him, I say."

Jim stumbled into his bunk that evening, muttering to himself, "Easy for you to say, Howard, but Esther was hanging onto Edgar's arm all afternoon. She didn't have ten words for me during dinner. Bah!"

*****

Pleasant summer days stretched into weeks, everyone on the boat happy in their jobs except Jim. He didn't understand his restlessness and boredom, a feeling he kept to himself as his savings account grew. One day Howard came aboard as his guest and sailed with them to Dockton on Quartermaster Harbor. The *Kalequah* was due for a few minor repairs at the boatyard, and her crew planned to take advantage of an early morning tide to dig clams.

The adventure was a new experience for Jim, and he was happy as he learned to dig steamers until his bucket was full. However, all the men on the tidal flats laughed at his consternation in "capturing" his first wild geoduck, its ugly neck stretched to more than a foot in length before its shell breached the sand at the bottom of a deep hole. The peculiar shellfish weighed less than Jim expected but was still three or four pounds – mostly muscle. "Who'd eat this gray wrinkled old sea monster? Why the last time I saw a sight like this overrated clam, it was called an elephant's trunk," Jim inserted jokingly as his friends razzed him. Howard replied between wheezing laughter, "Hee! Hee! But it's smaller than an elephant's trunk... Hee! Hee!" "Should I tell him what part of the elephant it looks like? Eh?" Ray joined the teasing, followed by all the men within shouting distance, stopping only when a local family walked out to the low water mark.

A clambake took place on dry land as the incoming tide flooded their clam beds, thirty or forty diggers boiling crabs and steaming clams. A couple of wives brought bread and potato salad to the impromptu picnic, with the Larsen brothers procuring two buckets of beer each from the Burton store. The owner and his wife brought a pot of hot coffee and a few cool bottles of sarsaparilla to the festivities.

Jim was gorging himself on the fine food when a familiar voice grated on his nerves again, Edgar's know-it-all tones announcing his presence, "My girl and I brought a couple of blackberry pies from my father's summer cabin up there. I hope you all like my baking."

Naturally the pair was invited to partake of the picnic food, somehow dimming Jim's jovial mood. *Ah well*, he thought, *I'd better be gracious. Besides, the tide has brought our shoreline back to normal. Time for us to row back to Dockton and take the Kalequah home.*

His friends willingly agreed when the clams and beer had been consumed, handing a bucket of saltwater containing four geoducks to the beleaguered Jim.

Howard took pity on his friend and suggested, "Let's take them home when we reach Tacoma. Tinky will clean them, and Momma will cook geoduck steaks for us. It's all right Jim, Esther and Edgar are staying on Vashon Island with his parents. Maybe we can run down to Old Tacoma and invite Uncle Carl. He loves geoducks."

*****

Two weeks later the *Kalequah* returned to Dockton for the installation of a minor part which had arrived from San Francisco.

During the brief afternoon layover, the crew was given free time, and Jim explored the village with Tinky trailing along. Jim's childhood nickname, "J.K.", was the subject of the lad's curiosity. "Tell me again why your family called you J.K. — can I call you J.K.? I think it's a good name," Tinky chattered as he skipped along the path beside his friend. "Of course you can, Theodore. I call you Tinky, don't I?" Jim replied with a comradely grin.

His buddy jumped with joy as they neared a gnarled root jutting across the trail, stumbling as his toe caught the obstacle and falling into a bramble of blackberry vines. His cry of pain was accompanied by a muttered, "Oh, I'm stuck. That was clumsy of me."

"I'll help you, Tinky. Here, grab my hand and I'll lift you straight up," Jim offered as he reached his left hand into an alder tree. They successfully eased the unfortunate lad from the thorny trap just as the frail alder snapped loudly, Jim's burden pulling him one way while the falling tree went the other. Jim's wrist was intertwined with the branches of the alder and stretched abnormally before it slid free. He fell backwards onto the path beside Tinky.

His lower arm was numb with shock but didn't seem a serious injury until his friend brushed his elbow in standing up. "Ayeeh!" Jim screamed in a flare of pain, at last realizing he was really hurt.

"I'm sorry, Jim," Tinky moaned in guilt. It was dumb of me to fall into that berry patch. Can you walk to the boat?"

*****

The clanking of the gangplank being pulled aboard the *Kalequah*, awakened Jim from a restful sleep, the engine coming to life at the same time. His memory of the Dockton accident was instantly brought to mind as someone touched the cool wet towel wrapped around his injured arm.

Tinky raised a half-glass of water to his parched lips, admonishing his friend, "Here, drink up. Tellie says fresh water is good for you."

"Uh, where are we?"

His partner and caretaker answered quickly, "In Gig Harbor, Jim. Ray couldn't find a doctor so Rollie is taking you to Point Fosdick. Does your arm hurt?"

"Hmm…yah…sure," Jim replied in fevered tones as he slipped into merciful unconsciousness.

*****

Jim heard Tinky's voice asking him a question but was too tired to answer until someone removed the towel from his arm. He screamed himself awake, more than a bit embarrassed to be such a baby as he found the crew's quarters full of his friends.

A sympathetic doctor advised, "Go ahead and yell, Mister Gerber. I'm Doctor Howlitz, and I'm going to set your broken arm before we carry you to the schoolhouse. Ah, here comes Mister Anderson with a bottle of local spirits. You know it's taboo on the reservation, but Howard had found a cache of the medicinal stuff for you."

Howard was panting as he handed the green-tinted bottle to the doctor and told Jim, "Drink up, Buddy. I'm helping this Olympia doctor to fix your arm before he goes home. Ha! Ha! Then I'm your nurse for a few weeks."

Rollie nodded and explained, "You'll stay with Howard in his room. Our medical expert doesn't think you should work aboard ship for a few months."

"But you can earn board and room as a handyman on the reservation," Howard continued, "And you can sit in my classroom while you're recuperating. Let us take care of you, Jim."

The patient began grinding his teeth on a stick of wood while the doctor removed the towel and bathed his arm, accepting a third big slug of liquor and muttering, "Go ahead, Doc. I'm half drunk already," and promptly blacked out at the first pressure applied to set his broken bone.

*****

The eldest pupil in the grammar school quickly overcame his chagrin at being so ignorant, sharpening his three R's in a few weeks of study. What followed surprised even himself, for once Jim started to read, every book in school, in Howard's small library, and in the agent's office was consumed with a delayed but voracious appetite. His widening vocabulary enhanced his conversational skills with history and geography a close second in achievement.

For class Jim wrote a poem about the Delaware River which was a literary flop and then a short story featuring his train trip to Tacoma. He was thrilled when everyone liked it.

For himself he wrote his mother a long letter on his life in Washington, opening an exchange of family news which lasted for a couple of years until she died suddenly of pneumonia. Steffi wrote the sad obituary, and brother-sister letters would continue for the decades to come.

Arithmetic was more difficult, somehow its abstract nature was forever a mystery to Jim, but he could handle money and navigate a boat, so he didn't worry about it. Jim was good at accumulating his wealth, hard work and frugality natural to the young man.

Working at every task given him by Howard and the clerk in the reservation office kept the one-armed handyman fit and active during the ensuing weeks. Doctor Howlitz pronounced his arm healed just before Christmas, took his splint off, and then continued on to Tacoma for the holidays. Jim's muscles were stiff with disuse, and it remained painful to exercise. Both the doctor and now Howard laughed off his complaints as "all in his head."

*****

Happily accepting the Andersons' invitation to spend the holidays in their home, Jim had fun shopping with Howard after arriving in Tacoma. He even raided his savings account, withdrawing a few dollars for the first time and leaving a balance of two hundred dollars in the bank.

Wearing a new shirt and carrying a sack of gifts, he walked beside his friend up to the now familiar house. It seemed more like home to him than any other recent residence.

Activities celebrating Christmas were a much appreciated repetition of the previous year. The Anderson women were friendly, Howard and Uncle Carl were buddies, and his college student nemesis was his annoying self. As Mary and Esther cleared the dinner table, the men shared a brandy amidst tales of the University of Washington and its stellar freshman, Edgar Randall.

"Jim, I think it's foolish to study with those Nisquallies in Howard's class. You're a sailor with a good job at Puget Sound Freight. That's not bad for a fellow like you," Edgar pontificated loftily as Carl refilled their goblets.

Howard and Carl glanced at Jim to see his reaction to the crude remarks, and the sailor decided to overlook Edgar's sneering tone. However he replied in kind, "Randall, you're a prissy fool, but I won't tell you to drop your education. Maybe you'll learn something about real people in your classes. Heck, I bet your father can probably make a banker out of you anyway."

Jim softened his comments with a chuckle and a not unfriendly slap on Edgar's back, the collegian, not sure whether to laugh or to curse, settled on the compromise of ignoring the criticism and continuing to describe college life in Seattle. Carl's foxy wink over the self-centered talker's head satisfied Jim's need for approval. He didn't have to take any verbal abuse or "better than you" attitude from anyone.

Still, Randall's remarks struck a nerve with the semi-invalid Gerber, and two days later he asked Howard to take a walk with him.

"Howard, am I a good enough student to attend college? What about that new University over at Ninth and Yakima?" Jim queried as they strolled through the park.

With a quizzical expression on his face, Howard glanced at Jim to see if he was serious. Ascertaining his friend's sober mood, he replied, "Yes, I think so. The University of Puget Sound isn't exactly new, just in a new location. It's not far from here. Why don't we go ask the Registrar – at least that's the fancy title my friend claims. I can put a good word in for you."

*****

The overcast sky grew darker as Jim gaffed his twenty-pound ling cod, and pulled its writhing form over the side of the eight-foot skiff. Thwacking the twisting fish between his bulging eyes with a billy club to still the movement stopped the wallowing motion of the small boat. Jim looked up with a sigh of exasperation as the rapacious riptide carried him away from Point Fosdick.

"That'll teach me to catch one more fish before I headed home. Four ling cod are a boatful, and they need cleaning. Maybe I can catch the eddy along the Tacoma shore," he muttered aloud.

Jim wrestled his oars into their locker and stroked for the bluff a hundred yards away. He was sweating with exertion, and his left arm muscles were aching when he felt the outgoing tidal flow release his skiff. He was drifting south in his eddy and in thickening dusk when he spotted the campfire on the shore and headed for it.

"Hello ashore! Can I share your camp for the night? I have ling cod cheeks and liver for a meal," Jim called loudly.

"You bet, fella. Your company and the cheeks are both welcome, but you can keep those damn livers – ugh!" the older man's voice carried through the night air.

A gray-haired muscular fisherman helped Jim drag his skiff high and dry, offering his hand in introduction, "I'm Oscar Miller, no relation to that fellow who once claimed this hillside. Are you from Point Fosdick?"

"Yes. I'm Jim Gerber. I appreciate your sharing this spot with me. Who does own the Tacoma Narrows anyway? I heard about a court case a few years back," he replied as he expressed his curiosity.

Oscar chuckled good-naturedly, "Who knows and who cares? It's a quiet campsite we are sharing. Let me help you slice the cheeks from your cod."

"I see you've got bacon and potatoes frying in the skillet. Sure you don't want to add livers? I hear its oil is good for you."

"Ha! Ha! No thanks," Miller avowed emphatically, "Ling cod cheeks are terrific eating. All we need is a good meal and a warm fire for tonight. You can cook your fish liver after supper."

Jim nodded with a smile as he suggested, "And a little conversation before calling it a day would be welcome."

Later the guest began gathering handfuls of madrona leaves and fir boughs for bedding in the dry sand. Oscar hastily warned his guest, "Watch out for poison oak, Jim. It's all through the brush along the hill."

Miller remained on his feet until he was sure the young man hadn't tainted their camp with the dreadful bush. When Jim settled his body on the improvised bed, Oscar followed suit, both men placing booted feet near the fire and resting their heads on a hummock of loose sand. Jim watched enviously as his companion spread a ragged but warm-looking blanket over his body and shrugged nonchalantly as he wrapped his jacket over his chest and shoulders and stared at the quarter moon drifting behind fleecy clouds.

At least it isn't raining, he thought dreamily. *Golly, I liked visiting that university with Howard, but I don't think I can go to school for three years. Maybe that's why that "Dean" fella looked down his nose at me – just like Edgar does. Howard got him to agree that I could enroll in September as a probationary student. If I do well enough I can be a regular student in the spring. I'll have to save more money if I attend such an expensive college.*

Of course, Mary Anderson approved of my venture while Carl and Esther were polite but doubtful. And as usual, Edgar jeered at the idea of my taking college classes, even belittled Puget

Sound as an upstart university. He deserved a punch in the nose, but I remained on my good behavior all vacation.

Hmm! Now I need a job. Maybe I'll go over to Fox Island and work in the clay factory. I can get plenty of exercise for my arm making bricks and save money to boot. And I'll take that job with Carl, fishing at Point Defiance in May. Maybe we'll go up to Friday Harbor for the summer, or maybe I'll see..., Jim drifted into an exhausted sleep.

*****

With a chorus of grunts, the volunteer crew of fishermen lowered Carl's eighteen-foot fishing boat into the water, laughing in camaraderie and accomplishment as they walked away. Jim placed a restraining hand on Carl's arm, offering, "You and Howard secure the boat. Tinky and I will help the Vranovich family put their boat into the water."

Carl nodded in relief, his age reflected in his weary expression. Tinky raced ahead, calling over his shoulder to his strolling buddy, "Come on, Jim. When Al's boat is in the water, Howard promised us a sarsaparilla. And his mother is cooking roast beef with potatoes and gravy for our farewell supper."

"Ha! Ha! Right you are, Tinky. Don't fret, we'll get our soda before walking up to Wright's Park," Jim replied cheerfully, his thoughts reverting to the events of the past month.

Golly, Rollie's going to work for the Hunt brothers at Wollochet Bay was a surprise. His replacement is grouchy and mean to boot, even if he is Maguire – no relation to Harry. Captain Maguire called Tinky a "Dummy" and fired him, and then Tellie quit and joined Rollie at Wollochet Bay. The Kalequah has become a different boat altogether, and I turned down my old job when Harry offered it to me.

Besides I'm going to college after I get back from fishing the San Juans with Uncle Carl. I'm sure I'll be happier with an interesting summer job – I hope we catch plenty of fish. Tuition is kind of expensive.

"Hey Jim, give me a hand with this confounded dolly," Al called from the yard behind the Vranovich home.

Jim grinned ruefully at his daydreaming manifestation, saying nothing as he helped Al slide the makeshift dolly under the eighteen-foot twin of Carl Anderson's boat. A half dozen men

appeared suddenly, and the craft seemed to glide down McCarver
Street to the Old Tacoma dock. The volunteers disappeared just as
quickly   minutes   later   when   the   boat   was   floating   on
Commencement Bay.

Tinky pointed out Howard and Carl walking up the hill
toward Thirtieth Street, and the two friends ran after them, carefree
and laughing now that the day's work was done. Tomorrow they
would begin a new adventure in the islands of northern Puget
Sound.

Chapter 5

Rain squalls battered the twenty-two foot open fishing boat as it plied the choppy waters of Colvos Passage, Ollala barely visible through a foggy mist. Carl maneuvered the broad-bottomed boat from his perch at the tiller behind their seine nets, the forward single sail billowing fitfully in a gusty wind. Howard, Tinky and Jim huddled in their oilskins on a pair of seats – neither wet nor dry, cold nor warm. Their only canvas was in use so they mouthed a joint prayer for a sunbreak to ease their discomfort, only Jim paying attention to their progress paralleling the Vashon Island shoreline.

"Hey Skipper, want me to spell you at the tiller?" Jim offered.

Carl nodded cheerfully in acceptance, "You bet, Jim, but wait until we clear Blake Island up ahead. How much 'sailing' experience did you bring from back East?"

"Not much! A couple of trips in Delaware Bay and once in Long Island Sound, but always with a real mariner in charge. I think I can handle this boat as long as the weather isn't too rough."

Jim's stint at the helm coincided with a blessing of sunshine and moderating seas, their boat scooting between Alki Point and Bainbridge Island through Elliot Bay, while avoiding the Seattle-Bremerton ferry as Ballard came into view to starboard.

A trio of gillnetters like themselves pulled away from the dock, Carl waving to their fellow fishermen as the newcomers paralleled their northerly course.

"That's Sven Andersen and his boys. Comes from Oslo and spells his name with an 'e', like many Norwegians. That's right, he's no kin of mine, but an old friend, nevertheless. Sven thinks he's a Viking, and heavy seas just another challenge to him. The Andersens will cross the strait to Friday Harbor in spite of this weather. Me, I'm more careful. The waters east of Whidby Island will be calmer today," Carl chattered.

Moments later he pointed south with an imperative finger, "Why, that must be the *Duwamish Queen* back there. Yep, loaded with gold miners, I expect. See her stack spewing smoke into the wind in front of Mount Tacoma. She's a rickety old steamship refitted in 1899 for the Klondike trade. Lots of prospectors still ride her up to Skagway seeking their fortune. Bah, foolishness I say. We'll make more money fishing for salmon this summer than most of them find in gold all year."

Jim smiled and quipped, "But those miners tell me it's fun when you strike a pocket of good nuggets. Heh! Heh! I agree with you, Carl, the prospect of freezing my butt all winter scares me. You seldom get something for nothing is my belief. I'm not much of a gambler – except at penny-ante poker maybe."

Carl nodded and resumed his seat at the tiller as Edmonds fell astern, his comment a bit grim, "There go the Andersens toward Port Townsend, with the *Duwamish Queen* behind them. No thanks, we're heading the other way around Whidby. Look at our skies: the sun is going behind storm clouds, and white caps are everywhere. Maybe we'll spend the night at La Conner or Coupeville if it gets too nasty."

*****

Carl skirted the brownish waters off the Skagit delta, a plethora of flotsam and jetsam drifting out of the river valley. As Carl set course for La Conner with dusk falling over Skagit Bay, Jim eyes spotted a fishing boat standing out from a nearby island. He pointed toward it with a brief question, "Is that Sven Andersen?"

Carl studied the other party for a moment before coming about, observing, "You have good eyes, Jim. That's Sven all right, and he's waving us over. I believe I see the *Duwamish Queen's* smoking stack behind Hope Island – must need help."

Five minutes later they were within shouting distance, and Carl bellowed, "Sven! Do you need something?"

"Yes! Junior and Marty can use your help caulking a few seams on the *Duwamish Queen*. That fool captain followed us across the strait in really rough seas. We pulled into Skagit Bay through Deception Pass – just barely made the tide. The *Queen* followed us twenty minutes later and fought both tide and wind. Actually scraped an underwater rock on the north shore. Lucky the hull wasn't stove in, but the steamship did spring a leak or two. Captain says he'll feed us if we lend a hand."

Carl agreed quickly, "Of course we'll help. With this weather we are going to lay over at La Conner tomorrow anyway. Lead the way to the steamship."

*****

Carl and Howard lowered a lantern float and gillnet over the stern. They untangled twists and knots in the ropes as the cork buoys bobbed away from the open boat and the lead weights took the lower edge deep into the water. Jim and Tinky observed the net-laying process as their oars steadied the vessel. They were in the lee of Lopez Island after traversing the choppy waters of Rosario Strait.

Carl threw a wooden keg over the side, marking the end of their gillnet spanning the channel. A local fisherman rowed his skiff away from the area, trolling toward a kelp bed near shore. Tinky's friendly wave was ignored as the fellow disdained any contact with "South Sounders."

The two veterans began pulling the net into the boat, methodically laying it over the floorboards in a reverse spiral. Jim's quizzical expression produced a terse explanation from Carl, "Our first setting is just practice. We'll do it a couple of hundred times this summer. You and Tinky can put it back in a minute – practice, you know."

A small silver salmon was pried loose from the net with torn gills, Howard dropped it on the floorboard as a smaller silver slipped through the four inch mesh. He grinned as he commented to the Checakos, "Fresh salmon for lunch, Tinky!"

As the last buoy was lifted aboard, Carl handed the net to Jim with nary a word as he took a seat and dipped his oar in the water. Howard and Tinky exchanged places also, and the newcomer practiced laying the gillnet before experienced eyes.

*****

The four fishermen slept under the protection of the spread sail, their bed but a blanket on the floorboards of the boat. Jim felt every twist and turn of Howard's restless body and every snore-snore-phewt from Carl's throat. They had dragged the craft high and dry on a sand beach to make camp for the night, and Tinky had roasted five spitted salmon over an open fire. Beans and salmon would be their daily fare in the days to come.

Carl's rough hand on Jim's shoulder awakened him in the pre-dawn hours, his amused voice ordering, "Come on,

Sleepyhead. It's time to go to work. There must be a school of fish running off shore – just for us."

Staggering to his feet after donning his now-dry boots, Jim went through the motion of eating half-warmed beans and drinking scalding hot coffee. It wasn't until he felt the cool spray of salt water on his face that he came fully awake, not unlike the new day as dawn beamed with a corona-like effect over Mount Baker.

By late afternoon all four fishermen were weary but happy with their lot. Jim was looking forward to sailing their cargo of forty-two salmon to Friday Harbor and a fish buyer. Carl smiled at his expectant crew even as he headed upshore toward their taciturn local fisherman. The fellow pulled in his lines and rowed vigorously to a rickety old dock situated before a sparse log cabin, arriving at his destination in time to grab Carl's bow line and tie it to a surprisingly sturdy piling.

"Howdy, Clem! Got my bacon? Potatoes? Bread?" Carl queried as he reached out to shake the man's hand in a friendly manner.

"Yup! Got a quarter of venison, too. Ready to trade?" a grizzled old-timer replied as he glanced at the youngsters with Carl.

A spirited bartering session ensued between the older men, Clem Brown coming alive with the interaction, his hazel eyes buried deeply under bushy gray eyebrows reflecting his pleasure. Jim guessed he was in his sixties with shaggy hair and unshaven face as gray as his brows.

Some sort of agreement was reached because Carl waved his crew forward to load the salmon in a sturdy wooden box at the dock even as the lively conversation continued.

Brown soon broke away from his almost social behavior to inspect his fish box and then led the crew to his cabin. His reclusive nature came to the fore as he opened the door and the flat of his hand stopped Howard from entering his home. Clem handed Tinky a flitch of bacon, Jim a gunnysack half-filled with potatoes and Howard a medium-sized tin of flour. Carl's eremite friend closed the door before leading the skipper to a smokehouse out back which obviously doubled as a meat locker. Clem produced a smoked salmon and a quarter of venison. Carl led the food cavalcade to his boat and stowed the supplies. A somber Clem untied the bow line and shoved the boat away, his stolid demeanor back in place.

Carl headed to their desolate beach once Howard raised sail, remarking, "Clem Brown is a regular hermit. He likes to be left alone in that old cabin – built during the Pig War, I hear. Hmm, I don't know of anyone who has seen the inside of his home."

"He's always friendly with you, Uncle Carl," Howard noted.

"Yes, he loves to barter, he's a man of his word, but he's just not sociable. He will smoke those salmon along with his own catch and sell the lot in the village at the north end of this island – called Lopez as well. He owes us some more meat and potatoes," Carl explained.

*****

Jim's initial glimpse of Friday Harbor was a scenic view of the idyllic island town and produced an almost romantic feeling like love at first sight. Carl was aware of the young man's reaction and quipped, "Prettiest sight in this country, Jim, and the islanders swear by it. However winter is west and windy, and the San Juans are lonely. My brother and I thought about fishing out of Friday Harbor, but Mary put her foot down. She loves her home by Wright Park."

After a momentary pause, Carl announced, "Let's celebrate in town tonight. I'll buy a meal and a drink – sarsaparilla for you,Tinky."

And so went the summer fishing season as the Tacoma gill-netter moved from Rosario Strait to Roche Harbor, Orcas Island to the Strait of Juan de Fuca, and all the islands within the San Juans. Jim's favorite spot was near Shaw Island, first because of a neat sandy beach used for overnight camps, and second because Friday Harbor was close enough for a quick visit now and again.

Plenty of salmon and steady prices made the four fishermen a happy crew, even a split sail failing to dampen their high spirits. They rowed into Anacortes one day to buy a new piece of canvas, selling their fish and sending money home to Mary. They enjoyed a Sunday in the small port, Carl picking up a stranded old Indian named Sollie. The Lummi Islander hitched a ride home in trade for a day's work and the location of a "secret" salmon run. Despite his aged, stooped body and a creased leathery face, his gnarled, sinewy hands were skilled in the art of gillnetting, and salmon filled their boat.

Carl laughed when Sollie's secret Lummi fishing spot turned out to be well-known to the fishing fleet. However, they humored the old-timer by spending an afternoon there and then trading their catch for a barrel of seawater full of clams, oysters and crabs, plus a few other supplies. Besides the friends made that evening, Sollie basked in the respect his tribal brothers gave him during the swap session.

Everyone was feeling good as Carl steered along the northern shore of Orcas Island, reaching Waldron Island in time to set up camp and a real old –fashioned clambake. Jim and his companions ate well over the next few days.

*****

On a visit to Friday Harbor to sell their catch and eat a boardinghouse supper, they were greeted exuberantly by Sven Andersen on the main street, his voice suddenly dropping to a loud whisper as his eyes swiveled about, "Carl, the kings are running heavy west of Stuart Island, and there are only a couple of boats in the area. I'm going back in the morning."

"Thanks Sven! We'll see you there," Carl replied as he slapped his friend companionably on the shoulder. He waved his crew to the dock area, manning their boat quickly and were under sail even as the sun dipped toward the horizon.

He grinned as he explained, "Sven's tips are worth real money, lads. We'll go up to Shaw Island this evening and camp. I want to be riding that tide near Stuart Island at daybreak. I think I know where the kings are running if they're still out there."

Jim understood Sven's optimism by the time they began picking up their second net, thirty-one "keepers" filling the bottom of their boat. Back-bending work felt good as gold when he and Tinky pulled on a full net, but suddenly their catch became an anchor and the tide swung their boat inshore.

"Careful men! We must be hung up on a reef or something," Carl shouted just as Tinky heaved the net free and the boat spun in a powerful eddy. The tangled rope threw Tinky off-balance and as he braced his foot on their cargo of salmon, he teetered out of control, flipping head over heels into the shallow waters when the hull crunched over a barnacled rock.

Jim lashed his rope over a cleat before he looked up, searching for Tinky until the lad's head bobbed to the surface twenty feet away. He answered Tinky's frightened plea, "Help!" by kicking his boots off and diving over the stern away from the gillnet. He swam strongly toward his friend's last position, a head showing but a moment still beyond his reach. Jim stroked in that direction for a count of five, and lifting his head to fill his lungs, he dove to the gravelly bottom and followed it until it shoaled off Stuart Island. Seeing no sign of Tinky in the ominous depths, he kicked to the surface and repeated his attempt, but the only person he found was Howard with his hand pointing upward.

As they surfaced Howard sputtered, "Help Jim aboard, Uncle Carl. I'll look for Tinky one more time."

Jim fell inboard onto the slimy salmon and squeaked, "Can you see anything? Has Tinky surfaced?" Carl's silence was his only answer, and when Howard grabbed the side, Jim knew his friend was gone.

Sven, his sons and three other boats came alongside and searched for an hour, trailing the outgoing tide without avail. The Andersen clan finally relieved Carl's boat and net of its salmon so Jim and Howard could bail seawater as Carl raised sail to follow the Andersens into Friday Harbor. After Carl notified local authorities of the accident and after Tinky was declared lost at sea, the old man's energy dissipated, and a hangdog attitude dominated his slumping shoulders.

"Uncle Carl, it wasn't your fault. It was an act of God you couldn't change. We'll all miss our young friend," Howard spoke in sympathy.

When he looked at Jim for support, he heard a half-hearted comment of agreement, "That's right, Carl! Tinky just slipped away. I wish I could have got a hold on him."

*****

The lights glowed along Seattle's waterfront, doubly colorful as its mirrored images shimmered over the rippling waters of Elliot Bay. Jim gazed into them with hypnotic comfort as he stood beside the packet's wheelhouse. The sorrow of his friend's death was abating, he had mourned for the past two days.

In his reverie he silently voiced his thoughts, *Carl's taking it harder than Howard and me. He's just moping in his bunk below. Claims he's through with fishing. Howard was more surprised than I was when he sold everything to Sven. He believes his uncle is seeing a repeat of the Alaska death of Howard's father and feeling very guilty.*

*Howard says we have to stick close to him while he's suf-
fering and depressed. I guess I'll go to our cabin and nap so
Howard can eat a bite. This boat docks at midnight, but we have
our bunks until daylight. We'll worry about catching a boat home
tomorrow. Maybe we could ride the train to Tacoma.*

Awakening in the uncomfortable chair where he had dozed
all night, Jim stretched his stiff muscles as he observed two empty
bunks. He opened the cabin door and stepped into the corridor,
stumbling upstairs in the direction of his friends' voices – Carl's
strident and Howard's patient. The morning sunlight framed
Seattle's skyline behind the arguing figures of his companions as he
interrupted with a peacemaker's purpose, "Well, are we going to
the shipping office next door or to the railroad depot over yonder?"

Both men replied simultaneously, Carl's clipped tones stating, "By boat, of course." and Howard's quieter suggestion, "By
train may be faster."

Carl pointed his finger imperatively at a sailing yacht and
asserted a bit loudly, "Our skipper says these folks are going to Gig
Harbor!"

Jim's gaze switched to the object of Carl's attention, recognizing the Helmsens' yacht a stone's throw across the water. His
friend Sharon was watching them and waved to Jim as she said
something over her shoulder. Waving casually in return, he shouted, "Hello Sharon! Is your dad going to Tacoma?"

"Hello, Jim! Did I hear your friend correctly? Do you need
a ride?" the girl answered as her father stepped onto deck.

Jim repeated his request, "Yes, we do. Captain Helmsen,
could you give us a lift to Tacoma?"

Nodding reluctantly after a second aside from his daughter,
Harold Helmsen replied, "Of course, Mister Gerber. Any friend of
Sharon's is welcome aboard. Come on over to the *Dream of
Tonstad.*"

*****

Jim ducked under the swinging boom as the sloop changed
tack coming around Browns Point, Carl at the wheel as Captain
Helmsen crewed for him. The young man sat on a bench beside his
friend, smiling at his cheerful manner as he handled the yacht.

The Skipper called out, "Jim, have you ever sailed a sloop?"

Carl laughed and interrupted, "Or an almost-sloop like the
Tonstad?"

Jim shook his head as he recognized the repartee and ongoing bantering between two old seamen. Harold finally explained his point, "She's single-masted, rigged fore and aft, and carries a mainsail and jib."

"But no spinnaker or topsail is aloft, Captain Helmsen. I concede she's a lovely yacht," Carl teased further.

Harold threw up his hands in mock consternation, quipping, "I've a spinnaker at home, Captain Anderson. I only use it on open waters. Our Puget Sound doesn't need a sloop to be full-rigged. What do you think, Jim? Are you a sailor or a college student in your answer?"

"Captain Helmsen, your wife and daughter call it a yacht," and as the patriarch grimaced forebodingly, Jim added hastily, "But I call her a sloop."

Harold nodded happily, stating in pontifical tones, "See Carl, we real sailors know a sloop when we see one. I'll add that spinnaker to her rigging when we sail up to Ketchikan next summer. Jim, Sharon asked if you and Howard could crew for us. Are you available?"

"Thanks for the invite sir. I wish I could, but I'm serious about college and I can't afford a vacation. Work, work and more work is my schedule for a few years," Jim responded in a mood somewhere between happiness and disappointment.

"Well said, young man. I spoil my daughter too much. Maybe you can convince her about college, either the University of Washington or a finishing school like Mills in California," Helmsen suggested casually enough, but Jim Gerber got the message. The Helmsens had money and Sharon was destined for the good life, and Jim was a poor struggling seaman.

*****

Uncle Carl blessed the memory of Tinky at the conclusion of his tale of the accident, supper growing cold as grief touched Mary and Esther as well. The grilled Olympia oysters were delicious, and Jim shook off his woe to say so, "Ladies, you've done justice to our seafood offering. Thank you for a tasty meal – as usual, of course."

"You're welcome, Jim," Mary replied before asking, "Do you men have to leave so soon?"

Jim nodded regretfully, "Yes, I do anyway. I have to visit

with friends at Wollochet Bay and see Tinky's grandma in Olympia. The *Kalequah* needed a substitute deckhand, and she sails in the morning."

Carl added, "Jim's taking a fish share to Grandma Tinker."

And then Howard chortled, "And visiting Sharon Helmsen in Gig Harbor. She was so thrilled when you asked her to supper, even if her daddy wasn't."

Esther eyed Jim in a new light as he blushed, but managed to respond lightly, "Howard spent more time with her on their yacht than I did, and he's the 'sailor' crewing for the Helmsens next summer. And who else was invited to supper?"

"And I thank you for that afterthought, Old Buddy, even if her father suggested it. Yes, I like Sharon, but she likes you," Howard stated with hope of denial in his tone.

Carl teased both young men, "Lads, you can romance Sharon Helmsen all right, but Harold has other plans for his daughter. Isn't that so, Jim?"

"Yes Carl, I realize he frowns on my friendship with his daughter, but he does seem to approve of Howard. Mister Anderson is more of a scholar and gentleman than me," Jim praised his friend with twinkling eyes – partly in jest everyone knew.

Esther laughed merrily, "Oh no, Jim, you can't get away that easily. Tell us about Sharon."

Chapter 6

Jim sauntered along Yakima Avenue, observing fellow college students entering the doors of the University of Puget Sound. His new clothes fit into the scene and bolstered his confidence on this opening day of school. He had registered the week before, as soon as he was paid by Harry Maguire. That day well-dressed young men and a few girls had looked down their noses at his garb – clean but working class.

Esther had taken him in hand and helped him spend more money than he wanted to, but he was unnoticed in the crowd today. As nonchalant as he looked, Jim was nervous, apprehensive of looking foolish before the awesome intellect at the university.

During registration he found that Dean Smith was neither the Dean nor did he have a doctorate. He was minister and professor of theology and was the authority who approved Jim's class schedule. Mature for a freshman, Jim knew well enough that he had to satisfy Professor Smith, so he went straight to the man for advice. Stern disapproval softened as they talked again, or perhaps the Acting Dean was replaced by an approving Professor. They both agreed that a medium class load was needed, with English composition, American history and world geography heading the list. An "easy" course in gymnasium and hygiene seemed appropriate, and a required class in theology was added. The latter course was taught by his advisor. James Smith proved to be human after all as he laughed at Jim's expression and then agreed to be his official "sponsor."

The new student walked directly to a small auditorium for an assembly of students and teachers. All the rear seats were filled by young men gathered in a clique, so Jim chose an empty seat near the left front. A slight and fair young man, boy actually, voiced a shy "Hello!" and Jim answered with a nod and a smile. His attention was drawn to the dais and a distinguished gentleman who began to speak, welcoming everyone to the new school term.

Half an hour later Jim cast a bored glance about the room, over a hundred faces reflecting like feelings as his neighbor whispered, "He's smart and a fine man, but he talks too much. I'm Henry Behring. You're new this year, aren't you?"

"Yes I am. Pleased to meet you, Henry. I'm James Gerber – call me Jim."

As heads turned their way, both students closed their lips and looked as attentive as possible. Jim thought, *I don't want to stand out today, and I certainly don't need a demerit – or whatever. Of course, it's nice to make a friend who might be able to show me the ropes.*

*****

As the assemblage was released to attend nine o'clock classes, a low-voiced jeer came from the rear of the auditorium, "Henry's a sissy," followed by a chorus of tee hees.

Henry blushed and shuffled his feet agitatedly, a touch of misery clouding his eyes as he met Jim's glance.

The sailor-turned-student put a hand on the lad's shoulder and held him in place. He found no resistance to his grip as he asked without criticism, "Who's the bully-boy? Can you show where my English class meets?"

"Jack Aherne picks on me all the time. I don't know what to do about it. Mother tells me no fighting, but I should punch him in the nose," Henry bemoaned as they walked down the hallway. Leaving Jim at a classroom door, he continued with an upbeat smile, "I'll see you in our ten o'clock history class. I hear that Aherne's clique is taking that course, too."

Jim nodded absently and entered the crowded classroom for his first lesson at the University of Puget Sound. The nearest open seat was at a front row desk beside a well-dressed but very plain young lady. His unasked question was answered in kind by a nod and a pleasant smile, and Jim took his place next to her.

In a small but friendly voice, she introduced herself, "I'm Mary Ellis. Are you in the right class? This is a freshman course."

Chuckling softly, Jim replied, "Yes. I'm James...er...Jim Gerber and I'm in my first year."

The professor's avowed intent was to outline the course and his requirements, but he lapsed into a lecture off and on. Jim wondered how and when to take notes, his frustration going unnoticed as the teacher meandered along. When their first assignment was being written on the slate board, Mary whispered, "If you like, I'll help you with your notes during lunch."

The girl blushed at her forwardness as Jim quickly accepted, "Thanks, Mary. You've got a deal."

Wow, he thought, *I've made two friends who are real students. Maybe I can do this "schooling" thing after all.*

*****

Jim stared morosely at his open theology text without focus, pensively considering telling Professor Smith that his family was Catholic rather than Methodist. *No, he thought, I'm of neither persuasion, and it shows. I'll just have to study harder to improve my mid-term C grade. Also, Henry and I will have to keep running every afternoon to get better than a C in physical fitness. All those rich boys play games often – probably at their fathers' athletic club. They only sport I'm good at is swimming.*

Henry got A's in everything else. He's a real brain. He's taught me good study habits and tutored me in history and geography. I earned a B- in American history and an A in world geography.

Mary has a straight A record, besides teaching me the English language and helping me in the library. I was happy with a C+, but she wasn't and told me so. I said I got what I earned and she did good. She stated she didn't do well enough if I couldn't use "good" and "well" properly. I guess that's why I agreed that she could run with Henry and me in the afternoon.

My friend didn't think Mary should form a trio with us. Since it's obvious he likes Mary, I asked him why shouldn't she run with us. He finally admitted he didn't want to look bad to Mary. He was bothered by Aherne's sarcasm and teasing whenever they passed the clique.

I suggested he punch Jack in the nose, but he only blinked behind a glassy stare in response. Maybe I'll have to tell Aherne to back off, but that wouldn't help Henry's pride much. Oh well, I've ignored Jack's evil eye and sneer so far, and besides I like his father Ed. I had a long conversation with him on Parent's Day and told Jack and his friends his Dad was 'okay' – as they say these days. I had a beer with him and Captain Trilby last week when I visited the docks. He and Rollie are old friends – a real compliment to Ed in my mind.

"Pst! Jim!" brought the young man out of his reverie. Esther was standing beside him and beckoning him into the hallway.

"You are attentive when you study – or daydream," she teased with a twinkle in her eye. "Momma wants you to pick up a bolt of material which your friend Harry has in his office. Can you do so on your way home?"

"Sure, Esther, glad to help. What's for supper tonight? Come along, I'll walk with you halfway home," Jim offered.

Esther agreed with a flirting smile, "Thank you, kind sir. Uncle Carl found a bucket of oysters he's sharing with us. Don't be late. Oh, here comes Henry and another boy to run with you."

"Hello Esther, are you running with us today," asked the other 'boy', Mary Ellis.

"Oh Mary, I didn't recognize you. I, uh, do you really run with these rascals?"

"Ha! Ha! Yes, even if my mother thinks it's not very lady-like. I like the exercise and the company. Why don't you try it?"

Esther was pondering the offer as she waved farewell to the trotting trio, now on their daily route around the campus.

*****

Jim left his companions on Yakima Avenue and trotted down Ninth Street to Pacific Avenue, wending his way through downtown Tacoma at a brisk walk. As he neared the Puget Sound Freight Company Office, he was confronted by Jack Aherne and his cronies. All four hoodlums rushed at him from behind a shed, grinning wickedly as they blocked his path.

"Gerber, you're a wise guy, and we're going to teach you proper respect for your betters," Jack sneered with relish.

Jim smiled and stood seemingly at ease as he answered, "If you have a bone to pick with me, Aherne, why bring a gang?"

Red and Zack charged at Jim, swinging fists indiscriminately. He stepped aside, brushed off Zack's clubbing fist, and pushed him against his buddy. Smiling still, he commented, "You don't like getting hit, Jack?"

He bloodied Zack's nose and banged Red's ear as he retreated to put his back to the shed wall, covering up as all four hoodlums pummeled him.

A police whistle trilled nearby, and a stentorian voice roared, "Round them up, boys. We have a cell waiting for these hooligans."

Jim grinned as he recognized Harry's voice, the four miscreants leaving the scene hastily. Chuckling wryly, he said, "Thanks, Harry. They've headed home, and I'm still in one piece. In fact, I'm well enough to take them on, but this time it'll be one at a time."

Harry laughed gaily, "My acting was pretty good, eh? Say, you're banged up some. Sure you want to go after them?"

"Yes, I know where they live, and I know they go home with Jack first – crowing, no doubt. I can run up Nineteenth and cross over Tacoma Avenue. I'm fast enough to catch up with them as they separate, and I can settle with them one at a time," Jim concluded in a confident tone.

Harry reminded the warrior, "Don't get in over your head. And remember that fourth lad was reluctant and only tapped you a couple of times."

"I know Harry. Jerry should find better friends. He's all right away from Aherne. I've talked to him about homework, and he's been helpful. Say, stick around and I'll be back to pick up Missus Anderson's bolt of cloth," Jim promised as he dashed away.

*****

Breathing heavily from exertion, Jim willed his lungs to quiet as he slid behind a fence adjacent to Jack's home. The alley entrance was secluded, and privacy was possible. He could hear Jack's strident voice boasting, "We put Gerber in his place. I wonder if he'll turn up for class tomorrow?"

A rafter of small talk followed as the boys headed for their separate houses, a crushing of gravel in the alley heralding Zack's approach. Jim raised on tiptoes and checked about him before launching his assault on the shuffling figure of his foe. He managed to slam his right fist into his foe's midriff before knocking him to the ground with his left shoulder. Jim straddled his surprised nemesis and punched him in the face at will.

"Enough! Enough! I give up. I'm sorry, Jim. Ouch my eye is closing, and I'm all bloody," Zack moaned in defeat.

Jim sprang to his feet and grasped his opponent's hand to pull him erect with a simple warning, "Leave me and my friends alone, Zack, and go wash your face before your mother sees you."

As Zack complied and hung his head abashedly, Jim trotted along the alley for two blocks before crossing over two streets. Here was where he came face-to-face with Red, who seeing Jim's fierce bloody face turned and ran for home and sanctuary. But Jim was faster and tackled his adversary in his own front yard.

Toe-to-toe fighting lasted but a couple of minutes before Red sank to the ground under Jim's onslaught, a crushed nose bleeding copiously over a split lip and a swollen eye. He kicked at Jim in frustration only to receive a bruising blow to his ear and his other eye.

He yelled "Uncle!" rather loudly and curled up in a defensive ball. Seeing neighbors looking on, Jim ran through Red's yard and up the alley for two blocks. He spotted Jerry crossing his yard and rushed forward. A totally shocked expression on his face, Jerry stood rooted in the grass when Jim accosted him.

Only the lad's mother standing in the doorway caused Jim to hesitate and to offer, "Want to take your punishment now or after?"

Jerry glanced bewilderingly left and right, shrugging as he raised his fists in defense. Jim reached inside his extended arms to slap Jerry firmly on the cheek, casually repeating the gesture on the other cheek.

A gasp from Jerry's mother was the only other sound heard as Jim asked, "Will that be enough, Jerry? We hit each other twice," and then offered the lad his hand to shake. With Jerry's nod he left before Momma could weigh into the fight. A flying mop missed Jim as he dashed down the street toward Jack's house.

*****

Dusk was falling as Jim walked onto the Aherne front porch, halting astride a wide welcome mat. He pounded firmly with the brass door knocker three times and waited patiently in place, not at all sure what to do next. The door swung wid, illuminating Jim's battered face in golden lamplight, Ed's greeting warm but hesitating, "Good evening, Jim, come inside…er…what happened to you?"

"Perhaps not, sir. I'm sorry to disturb your household, but Jack and I have a problem to discuss in the yard," Jim replied soberly.

The Aherne patriarch stood silent for several moments, studying his young friend. Breathing a sigh of understanding, he called over his shoulder, "Jack! James Gerber is here to see you."

Jack appeared immediately at his father's elbow, obviously listening in the front hallway. He glared his animosity at his visitor but remained silent. Jim finally asked, "Should we step into the yard and settle our differences with honor?"

"No," Mister Aherne stated firmly, "Discuss your grievance right here, Jim. There'll be no fighting in my home – or yard. What happened?"

Jack refused the challenge with his continued silence, so Jim spoke directly to the son, "I chatted with Zack, Red and Jerry. We have an agreement. You and I can discuss it tomorrow at college."

Ed asked his boy once more, "What happened?"

Jim interrupted politely, "I won't disturb your supper, sir. Good evening." He turned and walked away, breaking into a trot as he headed back to Harry's office for Mary's bolt of material and a bit of friendly advice – and some soap and water.

*****

Jim slipped quietly through the front door, only Carl noticing a cool draft of air crossing the dining room. He announced loudly, "Our wayward boarder is finally home. Let's eat, ladies!"

"Did you remember my package, Jim?" Mary asked as she shuttled food from the kitchen to the table.

A more curious Esther saw his face and blurted out, "Oh my goodness! James Gerber, have you been fighting?"

During the next hour Jim told an abbreviated story of his adventure, eating ravenously as he answered questions. He always seemed to have a mouthful of oysters when he didn't want to answer a question. The women finally cleared the table so Carl could beckon his young friend into the parlor and pour him a brandy.

"Shall we drink these spirits or bathe your wounds with the medicinal alcohol?" Carl teased unmercifully.

"Cheers, I say! I need a drink after my busy day."

"Come on, lad. Tell Uncle Carl the whole unvarnished story. I know you didn't get jumped by strangers, and skinned knuckles means you got a few licks in. Are we going looking for those hoodlums?" Carl queried as his fisted hand struck his palm.

From the dining room came a low but insistent order from Esther, "Yes, Jim, tell Uncle Carl now, but tomorrow you are walking me to school. And I'm joining you in the afternoon for a run. We're a quartet now."

*****

Surprisingly Mary pressed newcomer Esther to keep up with the men, Jim's quiet laughter completing the prompting. The quartet trotted along Eleventh Street heading toward downtown and then turned the corner on Yakima to return to campus. Five figures appeared ahead of them, stopping in their path. Jim recognized Jack Aherne and his cronies, whispering to Henry in an aside, "If there's trouble, Aherne is yours."

Suddenly Red turned heel and left the scene, and Jerry trotted across the street, heading into town. When he waved in a friendly manner, Zack guffawed and followed him.

Henry murmured excitedly, "All right, Jim, Jack is mine," and both men laughed at the humorous side of their situation as the girls listened with apprehension.

"I'll take care of his partner. Who is he?" Jim essayed and waved the girls to the rear.

Contrary to his orders, Mary and Esther picked up a handful of dirt and kept running, their burden of debris cast into Jack's face. Jim drove forward only to find the fifth gang member running away, Jack wiping his eyes and backing away from a belligerent Henry.

Esther called their attention to the unusual number of students in the area, many of them clapping in approval, "Look, Jim, everyone is cheering us. Jack made a fool of himself."

Jim voiced a unanimous opinion for the quartet, "That should end any more harassment. Let's enjoy our run."

*****

College studies seemed easier by Christmas vacation when Jim shared his progress with Howard and the Anderson family gathered for the holidays. An exchange of gifts emptied Jim's purse, but nothing could dampen his spirits at Christmastime. As the New Year 1902 was welcomed, Edgar's presence at dinner reminded Jim that Esther had a beau, the two youngsters taking a walk in the park after the meal.

Henry visited to tell his friends that Jack Aherne was a pariah in Tacoma's social circles. However, the news didn't raise Jim's morale. Without a word to anyone, Jim walked over to the Aherne house and banged the door knocker as he had a few weeks earlier, and Ed answered again.

Jim smiled at his friend's dour expression and said, "Happy New Year, Ed. Is Jack home?"

"What are you doing here, Gerber?" Jack snarled from the parlor door.

"I came over to wish you a Happy New Year and offer my handshake," Jim stated in as friendly tones as he could muster.

Ed's silence and quizzical glance at his son told Jim he'd patched up his quarrel with the father. *How about the son?* was his vagrant thought.

A dozen emotions crossed Jack's face as he glanced back and forth from Jim to his father, common sense finally dominating as he shook the extended hand and added grudgingly, "I'm sorry, Jim!"

Ed beamed with the holiday spirit of fellowship and offered, "Will you come in and have a glass of nog to celebrate the season? The Missus makes a tasty punch."

After Jack's nod of agreement, Jim accepted, "Just for a moment, sir. The Andersons are expecting me for dessert this afternoon. Jack, how are your classes going? All A's, I suppose."

Jack actually smiled pleasantly in the presence of his mother and sister and replied, "Not exactly, Jim. Your friend, Professor Smith, doesn't approve of me. I'll get a B from him for sure."

Chuckling, Jim confessed, "I think James Smith believes I'm a lost cause. I expect a C grade."

"Mom, Nancy, let me introduce my fellow student, Jim Gerber," Jack added in a solicitous manner, but with a smile as well.

"Missus Aherne, Miss Aherne, pleased to meet you. And thanks for the 'student', Jack. Ladies, I'm just a rough sailor in college and no match for students like your son and Henry Behring," Jim modestly acknowledged as he glanced into Nancy's twinkling eyes.

She inserted, "Mary Ellis is the best student at Puget Sound, and she speaks well of you, Mister Gerber. Can I join your running club when I enroll in the fall?"

"Of course!" Jim replied, accepting a glass of nog from Ed and then adding a toast, "As my father used to say, 'Prosit!' Have a Happy New Year."

He excused himself while he was still ahead, Ed's friendly hand on his shoulder well worth the effort he'd made to resolve their differences.

*****

The new term came in late January, Jim's bank account sadly depleted by tuition and board and room expenses. Professor Smith provided helpful advice, recommending he apply for a job in the lunchroom to help pay bills, and then insisted Jim toughen up his class schedule in the second semester.

Besides English literature, theology, and gymnasium, he enrolled in a five-hour course in biology which included two labo-

ratories a week – lots of work. Finally, he added a class he feared
greatly, freshman algebra.

Nevertheless, his determination to master the Liberal Arts
program resulted in good grades, including a C- in mathematics.
His running club earned him a B grade in gym as it picked up a
score or more additional members, Jack and his sister among his
companions all spring. In fact, Missus Aherne and Missus Tudor
had Jim to supper a time or two.

Mary had a crush on Jim, and Jim had a crush on Esther, but
everyone ignored the obvious and enjoyed their exercise hour.
Esther was still seeing Edgar, but in spite of a tiff of jealousy, Jim
couldn't dislike the Randall heir. His real worry was a profitable
job which would pay for next year's tuition.

Chapter 7

Jim stood watch as quartermaster on the *Dream of Tonstad*, Howard Anderson and Howard Helmsen tending the sails on the sloop. Sharon lounged near his friend, offering to lend a hand if the wind changed. *Golly*, Jim thought dreamily, *three strokes of good luck since my final exams. Professor Smith gave me an A in theology – a real surprise, as much as that B- in algebra. Then we went to the Dean's office where I was awarded a hundred-dollar credit on fall tuition and rehired as dishwasher in the lunch-room.*

Finally Harold Helmsen offered me a paying job as his mate on the family yacht. Here I am on "vacation" in the Strait of Georgia without a care in the world. Even Esther's engagement to Edgar didn't surprise me, nor have I suffered a heartbreak. I guess my crush on her was just a passing fancy. And Howard asked again about Sharon and me, and I repeated she's just a good friend. Those two sweethearts are becoming a "couple" – and Harold approves.

"Ahoy the helm! Is that Nanaimo off behind that island?" Captain Helmsen queried.

"Yes sir, but with this fine weather we should reach Campbell River by dusk," Jim replied.

"Is that the spot last night's fisherman told us about?" Harold wondered aloud.

"Yes, and tomorrow we'll sail in more confined waters to Port Hardy, the last village on Vancouver Island. I understand it's quite a voyage along the inland passage to Prince Rupert and then into Alaska Territory. Say Harold, are you planning to pan for gold in the creek at Ketchikan?" Jim asked with tongue in cheek, knowing the captain's opinion of prospecting.

The three sailors on deck chorused a hearty yes, the patriarch merely wagging his head on mock horror at the idea. Abigail and her two-year old daughter came on deck to join the camaraderie, Sarah in a harness tied to Daddy's deck chair as the playful conversation filled the warm and breezy afternoon.

*****

Jim heard the wind and rain in the middle of the night, aware the sloop was riding small swells easily in waters of Port Hardy. He slept in the next morning, expecting to ride out the summer squall, and was surprised by a shuddering roll of the sloop as it got underway. His only thought was a mild criticism of Captain Helmsen. *Why are we sailing in this kind of weather?*

Rushing topside to take the wheel from Harold, he shouted into the brisk wind, "What's our weather going to be like in the ocean, Skipper?"

Helmsmen waved to the blue sky overhead and optimistically shouted back, "Looks clear to me, Jim. We'll cross over to Fitzhugh Strait before you know it. Hold for Cape Caution while Howard and I trim the sails."

A hint of trepidation raised the hairs on the nape of his neck as he observed the local fishing boats still in the snug harbor. He worried aloud, "But Harold, none of the fishermen are coming out today."

"Oh Jim, it's Sunday and those fellows are all in church. We should be in lee of Calvert Island by noon," the Captain replied with confidence.

A cross between a nod and a shrug was Jim's only response as he took advantage of the favorable southwest wind for the next hour and a half.

Graying skies were the first sign of trouble, and freshening winds shifting to the northwest confirmed Jim's premonition of heavy seas. Harold called for less sail, ordering his family into the cabin as he and Howard Anderson worked the canvas. He signaled Jim to quarter aport and tack around Cape Caution as best he could.

Two hours of diminutive progress found the yacht a mile off the promontory and shipping seawater regularly. While it washed across her deck to drain out her scupper, Jim worried about a small percent that found their bilge. Anderson was an enthusiastic operator of the hand pump emptying the bilge. The Helmsen boy slipped onto deck, eager to help the men, only to have Daddy chase him below.

Harold relieved Jim at the helm, the latter transferring his rope cuff to Helmsen, a safety device for the sloop's quartermaster. Jim wrapped another line around his left wrist before standing aside. The Skipper shouted into his ear, "Good idea, mate. Stand by while I bring the *Dream* about into the wind. We're too close to Cape Caution for my comfort. Another mile or so and we can use the same wind to run for the protection of Calvert Island."

Jim nodded in agreement and braced himself as their vessel plowed into ten-foot breakers, clanging her way away from the headland – and from peril. Both men glanced aft to gauge their progress, ignoring their bow crashing into the chest of a heavy wave. The sloop swung wildly askew as she struck a crosswave. The cabin door banged noisily, and young Howard's cry for help merged with its clatter, the sounds carrying clearly with the oncoming wind.

Jim's eyes swiveled about to see the Helmsen lad slide across the deck on a sheet of rushing water, his momentum and the deck's tumbling action washing him over the side.

"Hold your course, Skipper," Jim yelled as he leaped overboard, his left fist grasping the safety line as he searched for the boy. In the tumultuous sea a moment of good fortune occurred, the brave young Helmsen son popped to the surface but an arm's length away. Before the next wave struck the sloop, the two swimmers merged, Howard wrapping his arms around his rescuer's neck while they pulled themselves to the sloop. Howard Anderson was on hand to pull them both to safety, no argument needed for young Howard to scurry into the warm cabin.

But Jim could not be spared from the next two hours of hard work, all three men required to sail the sloop into a quiet cove on Calvert Island. Two days of repairs and rest were necessary before the Helmsen sloop could cruise onward.

*****

Fate smiled on the *Dream on Tonstad* as it plied the waters of the inland passage of northern British Columbia, Harold cautiously following local fishermen through Seymour Narrows on a high tide – Ripple Rock no threat that day. They sailed at a leisurely pace through scenic Canada, Jim completing the last hurdle by successfully navigating the fjord-like Grenville Channel during daylight hours.

Everyone voted to skip their planned stop at Prince Rupert and cross Dixon Entrance in sunny weather. Dusk was falling as they maneuvered into Ray Anchorage on Duke Island and dropped anchor. They were in Alaskan Territory and had the splendorous frontier to themselves.

Harold and his son were up early, enjoying bountiful fishing while Jim and Howard took the dingy ashore to hunt deer with

Helmsen's rifle. The pair of hunters saw little in the dense forest
save animal spoor and one old black bear who chased them out of
his berry patch.
      Upon their return to the sloop with empty hands, young
Howard brayed shrilly, "Skunked!"
      Jim sheepishly agreed, "That's right, folks! But who wants
to eat stringy and greasy bear meat, eh?" The lad's only response
was to hold up a fifteen-pound King and grin his triumph. Needless
to say, everyone ate salmon all the way to Ketchikan.

*****

      Ketchikan labeled itself the Gateway City for good reason.
The inland passage was a calm voyage from Tacoma compared to
the perilous route over the ocean to Sitka. The bustling waterfront
on Tongass Narrows supplied many prospectors and fishermen in
the southeast panhandle of the territory. Its own creek of gold produced only minor wealth compared to Joe Juneau's northern find in
1884. The small settlement established that year became the incorporated town of Ketchikan in 1900.
      Aside from modest production of gold, local industries of
timber and king salmon ensured the community's growth. Sea
transportation through the small port added a respectable income to
the city's coffers as well.
      Harold pointed to the shacks along Creek Street, the precip-
itous mountainside necessitating buildings be built on pilings over
the water. He explained, "Ketchikan means 'spread wings of an
eagle' in the local dialect. Those houses perch along the shoreline
like eagles in a tree. Ha! Ha! My cousin Dag Helmsen has a general store here, and Dad is part owner. Our trip is a mixture of business and pleasure, and our ballast coming north are hardware items
– a lot of nails and bolts mainly. Hopefully, we'll replace them
with gold dust and canned salmon for our return trip."

*****

      During the ensuing days of leisure Jim strolled the streets
and boardwalks of the frontier town, absorbing the ambiance of the
territory and its gold rush culture. His ready smile and genuine
interest in Ketchikan's activities earned him an invitation from two
miners to pan for gold on their claim on the creek. Three hours

later he turned over a smattering of dust to the men and went his way thinking that prosperity was sure hard work.

Later that day Jim helped a gnarled and wrinkled old man carry his catch of salmon from his boat to the fish buyer, earning himself a day of fishing in Tongass Narrows with the taciturn Tlingit.

Jim lost track of the days and the Helmsens as he enjoyed his "vacation" and suffered a bit of melancholy when Harold concluded his family business/visit was over and announced their morning departure for Winslow. During the middle of the night he awoke to a clatter overhead, and after donning clothes he joined the captain and his family on deck where cases of canned salmon were being loaded as their ballast. One crate was taken into the cabin and stashed under Harold and Abigail's large bunk.

In the morning Jim met a new hand who would accompany them to Bainbridge Island. No questions were asked as the newcomer wore a holstered Colt .38 at his waist. Harold lowered his voice to introduce Marshal Halgreen. The officer nodded pleasantly and said, "Forget our late night delivery, mate. Let's sail to Winslow without any problems."

And so the *Dream of Tonstad* cruised out of Ketchikan, crossing Dixon Entrance and plying friendly Canadian waters. Unfortunately, the Marshal was seasick as soon as they left the dock, but fortunately their passage was smooth and problemless, so he wasn't needed. Harold breathed a sigh of relief as he spotted his father on the Winslow dock, happy to be rid of the gold and its "protector."

*****

Jim strolled down Pacific Avenue, lost in thought and feeling a bit lonely. He had returned to Tacoma by ferry and train in solitude, Howard remaining in Winslow to clerk in the Helmsen general store.

Boy, is Howard ever serious about Sharon and vice versa. And her father approves. He'll spend the next few weeks with them before the Point Fosdick School term begins.

I wish I had an option or two for work the rest of August. I visited Harry Maguire on the docks, but he didn't have a job for me, and neither did his brewery friend over by Gallihan's Gulch. Hmph! My bank balance and Alaskan wages will last me through Christmas, but I would like some spending money for this fall.

His reflective mood was disrupted by the familiar teasing voice of Jack Aherne, "Still a daydreamer, eh Jim? Got a minute to give me a hand with this crate?"

Jim smiled his reply as he turned to face the Aherne progeny, noticing Jack was leaning against a weighty-looking box on a dolly facing the steep slope of Nineteenth Street. He waved casually before putting his shoulder into the other side of the freight consignment, the pair pushing their burden up the hill to the loading dock on the alley.

Taking a breather, Jack gasped with a sly smile, "Whew! Thanks, Jim. How was yachting to Alaska? And pretty Sharon?"

Jim shrugged a noncommittal reply, "Fine, I guess. Decent wages, good food, and I only fell overboard one time. What's this about Sharon? How did you know about my job?"

"My sister visited with Esther Anderson and heard a lot of girl talk, or gossip if you like. I guess you know that Esther and Edgar are engaged," Jack reported with a sober demeanor.

Jim laid a hand on Aherne's shoulder in friendly acknowledgement, laughing as he commented, "Ha! Ha! Yes, and Howard Anderson is thick with Sharon Helmsen. He's visiting at her family home for the rest of the summer. My friend, they are both lovely girls, but not for me obviously."

His last remark and self-directed humor touched his former antagonist as he responded, "Thanks for being my friend. I owe you," and pausing he added, "How about helping me unpack this crate of dry goods, and we'll get Dad to buy us a beer."

Jim's hopes were answered as that social beer led to a job for August, unloading freight, stocking shelves and delivering orders – all respectable chores for the college student.

*****

The next morning Jim swept the floor of the delivery room on the second floor and for lack of instruction, he did likewise to the loading dock outside. Jack arrived late and hurriedly showed the newcomer the ropes, explaining Jim's duties to him.

"Jim, you're a jack of all trades. As floor boss I'll give you work, but so will every one else in the business. Now take these three packages down to Puget Sound Freight for delivery to some South Sound customers. Oh-oh, here comes a large delivery of goods for us. I'll meet the wagon, but hurry back to help out," Jack ordered.

Jim took his delivery to Harry on the double, apologizing to his friend for not chatting. He raced up the hill to help with the crates from the overloaded dray. Nathan was an old-timer on the second floor who preempted the task of stocking the shelves nearby. Jack carried a small carton downstairs, leaving Jim the job of moving the remaining five crates to the third floor on the decrepit lift in the corner shaft.

The upper floor was bossed by an elderly lady named Edith who was quite nice but remained at her cubicle office all the time Jim unloaded crates. She called for the bills of lading, "Please, Mister Gerber, bring those papers to me. I understand you just started work today."

In walking over to hand Edith the bills, Jim saw she was seated in a wheelchair, and quickly felt guilt for his unkind thoughts about her sitting in the corner, offering hastily, "Ma'am, can I move these crates closer to the shelves?"

"Why thank you, Jim. I'll tell my brother Ed that you are a fine worker. Are you a friend of Jack's from college?" Edith inquired.

"Yes, ma'am. I'll start my second year in a few weeks. School is expensive, so I'm glad you can use me. Where do these crates go?"

"Hmm, let me see…bring that big crate over here, then take the other four down the last aisle to the front of the warehouse. Isn't there a small package with this shipment?" Edith puzzled rhetorically.

"Jack took one such box downstairs after sticking its invoice on the big crate – right there, ma'am. I'll move the crates now."

Jim picked up the lightest item and carried it away, soon spotting a slight figure wearing a stocking cap and burly sweater – a ragamuffin outfit for sure. He approached the fellow and set his burden on the floor, asking, "Say fellow, where do I … er … Nancy?"

Before his eyes the slim lad had turned into a very pretty girl, upsetting Jim's social graces as he blushed a bright pink.

"Ha! Ha! Jim, you should see yourself now. I got you, didn't I? I've never seen you flustered before," Nancy laughed, enjoying his discomfort at his gaffe.

Jim grinned in self-ridicule as he replied, "So I'm silly," and with a delayed attempt to save face he added, "But who would expect a pretty girl in this place."

His compliment succeeded quite well, silencing Nancy as she blushed in surprise and stared soberly at the young man. Finally she flashed a brilliant smile of approval and stated happily, "Thank you,, kind sir!"

A period of mutual regard and diminishing blushes followed, Jim offering, "Can I take you to lunch, Nancy? I'd like to hear about your summer and college plans."

Beaming with pleasure, his friend made a suggestion, "I brought a lunchbox with me. Can we meet here by my favorite window and watch Tacoma's busy port while we chat?"

"Sure, come to think of it, Mary made up a box lunch for me. Maybe we can share goodies. What time is our lunch hour?"

"Hee! Hee! We only get a half-hour for lunch, Jim. Just come up when you're free." She hesitated as she added, "Would you invite Aunt Edith to join us? She is…"

Jim nodded in understanding, cutting her off with an "Of course! Hmm, maybe she'll tell me a few stories about the childhood of Nancy Aherne," Jim mused as he ducked a pincushion aimed for his noggin. He walked away in a happy mood, realizing he didn't feel lonely anymore.

*****

Jim enjoyed the established pattern of his summer job, daily lunches in the loft with Nancy and occasionally including her aunt and Friday after work with Ed and Jack at the local tavern. Somehow the two activities were exclusive of each other, neither Nancy nor her menfolk mentioning one another, and Jim was averse to acknowledging that romance was in the air.

One trait he recognized in his quiet-spoken friend was her strength of character. She said what she felt and could be more forward than the reticent Jim. He wasn't surprised when she invited him to Sunday dinner, "Can you come to the house at noon? Mother always has her meal on the table at two o'clock."

Recalling Jack's casual description of his family's Sunday routine, Jim accepted and offered, "Thank you, Nancy. Would you like me to escort you to church services? That is, if your parents wouldn't object."

"Oh Jim, you're a dear. I didn't know how to ask. My mother would be most impressed." Nancy rose to her tiptoes and kissed his cheek in appreciation. In turn, Jim leaned over and brushed her forehead with his lips.

"Well Nancy, let's hope my abstinence from church isn't noticed. I'd hate to embarrass you," Jim concluded with a whimsical expression.

*****

Spending a day with the Aherne family was a pleasant experience for Jim, who was reminded poignantly of his own family life before his father's death. Wearing his Sunday best and behaving with a quiet demeanor during the Methodist service avoided any problem, for which he was rewarded by Nancy with her affectionate smile as they walked hand-in-hand to the Aherne home. Conversation before and during a roast chicken dinner was erudite, Jim realizing the Ahernes were educated as well as socially prominent.

Following a dessert of strawberry shortcake, the three men retired to Ed's den for a brandy, a discussion of yachts, sailing, Alaska and Jim's work as a seaman proving amiable. However, the subject turned to an interrogation-like review of Jim's character, family and prospects as a suitor, amusing Jim until Jack mentioned his lunches with Nancy.

"I don't think spooning with my sister while working for the Aherne business is appropriate – no offensive intended, Jim. Nancy's kind of young and impressionable," Jack asserted in his usual aggressive manner.

Ed interrupted hastily, "We like you, Jim, and Nancy's entitled to her own friends. You're always welcome in our home."

Jim bit his tongue in silence, recognizing his friends' sincerity and well-meant comments even while they were being snobbish. Nodding in understanding, he replied carefully, "Ed, Jack, I don't see any problem. The University term starts in a week or so, and I have to leave the warehouse job anyway."

Ed sputtered, "I'm sorry,Jim, we didn't mean to offend you. We're just worried about Nancy."

"That's all right, Ed, I'll pick up my wages tomorrow and go pay my college bills," Jim stated with a smile covering his hurt feelings. Somehow Harold Helmsen's disapproval crossed his mind. *Hmm, I'm a good enough worker but not a proper suitor.*

Jim's pride forced him to exit the Aherne home without revealing his unhappy thoughts although he did feel a little like an actor and an escapee as he hurried home.

Chapter 8

Trotting along Yakima Avenue by himself allowed Jim to indulge in a bout of daydreaming. *Golly! My legs are tightening up already. I'm glad I got started a day before Henry and Mary could join me. It was good seeing them hand-in-hand at registration this morning; those two "students" are made for each other – another romance in the making.*

I said good-bye to Nancy in her father's office, leaving her puzzled at my abrupt departure. Ed shoved her out before she could ask any questions although he did tell me she was enrolling at the University tomorrow. I wonder what I should say to her about that conversation in the Aherne den – nothing is probably best.

Professor Smith talked me into taking geometry and ethics, and I insisted on my gymnasium class again. Along with American literature, world history and theology, I have a full schedule. Somehow I'm not excited about college this fall. I'm looking forward to reading and history, and of course my running club. Physical exercise keeps me sane, and I love to read, but I feel like I should be doing something – like real work.

I wonder if the rumor is true, that my alma mater is moving again. Professor Smith said he hoped not, so I expect he doesn't know either. He did say there are plans to require four years of study for a degree. Yah, just when I'm struggling to manage three years of college.

Maybe I can work at Puget Sound Freight during the Christmas holidays to earn my spring tuition. That money I sent Steffi yesterday wiped out my reserve. I hope Sis can help Momma get better during her visit. Ma's not getting any younger.

Jim heard his name called as he crossed Sixth Avenue, slowing to walk as Esther joined him through Wright Park, chattering with her engagement plans and "wonderful" Edgar. *Ugh!* he thought as he smiled and nodded in consonance with her diatribe.

*****

Henry and Mary waved good-bye as they turned off Ninth Street to go home, the light sprinkle of rain not deterring Jim. As he approached Yakima Avenue, he cut across the street to the corner. Nancy left her niche in a store front to run beside him in silence.

Between puffs of breath he asked companionably, "Did you get signed up for classes today? Hey, aren't you supposed to be working?"

Nancy cast a scowl his way, tersely retorting, "Yes! But why shouldn't I quit? You did! What's going on, Jim?"

A tear in her eye caused Jim to avert his glance, silent as they ran side by side, unable to think of a good explanation. He wouldn't lie about Sunday's talk in the Aherne den, even as she persisted, "What did my father and brother say to you after dinner? Aren't you welcome in their house?"

Hearing a question he could answer truthfully brought up a quick response from Jim, "No, I'm welcome at your home, Nancy. Er, don't you think you're a little young for me?"

Not realizing she was being diverted from her question, Nancy responded, "Dang it, Jim, I'll be seventeen years of age next month. Several of my girl friends are married already. Age isn't important. I think you're...ugh!...you're terrible," she muttered amidst tears as she left his side and headed home.

In the ensuing days she ran with twenty or so members of the club, sat next to him in their world history class and occasionally ate lunch with him before his shift started. Jim was relieved the argument didn't interfere with their friendship but did feel a pang of jealousy when Nancy attended social affairs which he couldn't afford.

The Andersons sensed his unhappiness, Howard asking about his love life, Esther hinting coyly that Nancy liked him, and Mary offering motherly advice on courting and social behavior. Only Carl earned an answer when he point blank asked, "Why are you such a grouch? If you like this Aherne girl, just tell her so."

In confidence he told his friend about that fatherly talk with the Aherne men, generalizing his conclusion, "They called me a friend, but just not good enough for Nancy. I'm broke and not likely to ever be rich. I guess they're right. I mean I'm not much of a prospect for the Aherne daughter."

"Well James, telling her about your feelings shouldn't hurt anything. You don't owe her family anything except courtesy and respect," Carl stated pontifically.

Jim wagged his head and crowed, "Ho! Ho! And who are

you to talk, Uncle Carl. You've never told Mary how you feel about her, have you?"

Carl blanched before his cheeks turned red, muttering a Norse epithet as he playfully pounded Jim's shoulder. He had no ready answer for Jim's cheeky rebuttal.

*****

Howard came home from Point Fosdick for his mother's surprise birthday party, Edgar and Jim joining the Anderson family in celebration. The warmth of the gathering was moving, even Edgar sensitive enough to behave properly. After cake was served Carl stood up suddenly and tinkled his wine glass with a fork for attention.

He smiled nervously and cleared his throat twice before speaking, his words taking a moment to sink in, "I have an announcement to make...er...Mary is a wonderful woman. Uh, I love her and asked her to be my wife." In surprised tones he concluded, "and she said yes."

Clapping her hands, Mary added, "Well said, my dear," and of her children she asked, "Will you give us your blessings? Howard? Esther?"

"Of course, Mother!" her children answered in unison, followed by congratulations from everyone.

Howard offered, "I'll go over to Sixth Avenue and find a bottle of champagne for a proper toast. Besides, Uncle Carl drank all that red wine getting his nerve up for the announcement."

The gathering was still chuckling as Howard, Edgar and Jim left the house in search of a bottle of spirits. At the general store they were abashed when they pooled their coins and found their combined cash would only pay for another bottle of red wine.

Jim good-naturedly joshed his friends, "You know why I had a single dime in my pocket, but Howard, you are employed, and Edgar, your father is a banker."

The eavesdropping storekeeper was genial enough to offer, "Howard, your credit is good. I don't have champagne but this expensive wine can go on your tab."

"Oh thanks, Mister Meikle, but we'll pay what we can afford. It's a gift for Mother and Uncle Carl – an engagement toast," Howard replied.

The elderly businessman accepted the coins from Howard

and then exchanged the cheap red wine for a Rhine wine from Worms, commenting, "Give your folks my best wishes. When are you getting married to that sweet girl who was with you this summer?"

Howard boldly forecast, "In December if her parents give their blessing and if my friends here will act as ushers at the wedding. Uncle Carl has agreed to be my best man. I hope you and your wife will come to our Tacoma reception at Momma's house, Mister Meikle."

The trio was strolling back to the Anderson residence when Edgar muttered, "You devil, Howard! Esther and I were planning our wedding for December. How can you gentlemen be my ushers if our dates conflict?"

Jim smiled at the raillery between his two friends, wondering how he could afford three weddings this winter. He thought he might just accept Uncle Carl's offer of a loan, even if it was to buy the Anderson clan wedding gifts.

*****

Leading his running club in front of the University, Jim pulled up when Esther waved a letter at him from the front steps. He called out, "Carry on, Henry. I'll catch up later."

Esther handed him the tattered envelope, stating, "Momma said to bring this letter from your sister Steffi. May I stay while you read it?"

"Of course, Esther, let's sit on these steps here. Hopefully my mother's better."

Jim hastily tore open the flap and extracted two pages, spreading them over his lap, tears soon splashing on the paper. Eyes glistened in sorrow as he read the entire contents before handing it to his friend with a brief prayer, "God rest her soul. Momma passed away two weeks ago."

"Oh Jim, I'm sorry, my mother sensed it was bad news. May I read Steffi's letter?"

The two friends sat with their heads bowed, Esther's tears joining those of the bereaved son. She looked up and spoke over his head, "Jim's mother died."

Jim felt warm arms encircle his neck, a tender kiss on his cheek creating a warmth in his soul as Nancy crooned her sympathy to him. He laid his head on her shoulder and cried silently, his grief assuaged by her gentle touch and loving serenity.

Jim followed Ed and Jack into the Aherne den and perched on the same chair he'd used on his last visit. As expected,Louise's meal had been delicious and on time, with entertaining conversation amongst the family. Her guest felt welcome and Nancy almost relaxed. A meaningful look between mother and daughter produced a bustle of activity cleaning the table, and the three men escaped to Ed's room.

The Aherne patriarch repeated the family's condolences, "We're sorry to hear of your mother's passing, Jim. In Pennsylvania, right?"

"Thank you, Ed. Yes, I come from the Scranton area," Jim replied soberly, pausing but a moment to change the tone of their talk, "Nancy was a true friend when I heard from my sister, and I realize I care very much for her. I guess I'm declaring here and now that my intentions are honorable, and I intend to court Nancy. I'm not very good with fancy words or manners, so pardon my straight talk."

Ed replied, "We're not offended by your declaration, Jim, but I don't believe your prospects are very good right now. You still have a couple of years at the University, don't you?"

Jack blurted out hastily, "And what about Samuel Gerrity? He has a bright future and he's calling on my sister. The Gerritys are a fine Puyallup family."

"Well that's for Nancy to decide, isn't it?" Jim responded with a poker face. He thought, *Who the hell is Samuel Gerrity? Nancy's never mentioned that name.*

Rising to his feet to end their little talk, Jim said, "Pardon me for leaving early, but I promised Mary to take her for a walk before I return home. Just a stroll around the block will do."

Sputtering in confusion and a bit angry, Jack failed to object before his father replied, "Go right ahead, Jim, but don't get caught in a rain shower. Maybe Nancy should take an umbrella. We'll see you at the Randall wedding next month. Nancy tells me you two are part of Edgar and Ester's ceremony."

"Yes, sir, and good day!"

Professor Smith failed to show up for class one late November day, his friend the ethics teacher dismissed his class without any assignment. As the students escaped through the open classroom door, Professor Adams hastily called out, "Oh...James, I have an errand for you. Professor Smith would like to see you. Can you visit him this afternoon?"

A puzzled Jim accepted a slip of paper from Adams, replying, "Yes, sir, is this address where Mister Smith lives?"

"Yes, and you may skip ethics. I'll give you some make-up reading next week. James is quite ill, so don't burden him," Professor Adams offered his advice with a fretful expression.

Searching for Esther in the library with success, he motioned her into the hallway, explaining, "Professor Smith is ill, and I have to visit him. Will you tell Henry to lead our running club today? And tell Nancy why I can't meet her afterwards?"

With her understanding nod and casual "Sure!" he left the building and hurried into a wintry drizzle – a snowflake falling hither and yon. His long strides down the Ninth Street hill brought him to Saint Helens Avenue in a few minutes. He turned left at the corner and slowed to check the number in Smith's address. A half-block away he found the correct number and entered a small lobby, an elderly lady waiting for him in the open doorway to the rear.

She impatiently waved him forward, whispering loudly, "Are you James Gerber, come to see the Professor?"

At his agreeable nod she stepped aside and remonstrated, "Don't keep him up too long. He needs his rest," and then slipped into the neighboring apartment.

Jim observed his teacher ensconced in his rocking chair in the corner, bundled to the throat in a great blanket. He studied the Professor empathetically for a moment before stating, "I see you're not well, sir. I'm sorry, how can I help you?"

Smith replied normally, "Thanks for coming, Jim. I need a favor and thought of you. Could you teach my theology classes for me until the Christmas break? My rheumatic heart is acting up again, and my doctor has ordered me to bed for a month. *Hmph!* One can only spend so much time flat on one's back, wouldn't you agree? Anyway, I'm sort of following his orders."

Jim's expression was dubious as he protested, "But I'm not a teacher. Besides I have a full course of study. There's several conflicts between our classes."

Smith checked his denial with a raised palm, commenting, "Ben Adams has the President's ear and can rearrange your sched-

ule if necessary. You won't have any problem teaching my eight
o'clock and two o'clock classes since you just completed that
course last year. Just follow my lesson plans and your memory. I'll
pay for your time, of course."
        "Oh no, I'm in your debt and can't take your money. All
right, sir, show me how I'm going to do this teaching thing."
        James Smith sighed in relief, thanking his friend, "I appre-
ciate your help, Jim, I'll be back in class after the holidays, and I'll
handle the course review and final examination. I suggest you take
command of my classes with a week's review and exam. That will
get our students' attention. Can you assign term papers?"
        "Yes, and require they be turned in before vacation. That
way I can correct and critique them for your grade. Will you be up
to reading a stack of papers?" Jim asked in teasing voice.
        The Professor chuckled and gibed in return, "Afraid you'll
have to grade them yourself?" and then commented more soberly,
"Ben Adams agreed to cover my Advanced Theology Seminar.
Those students are Divinity majors and represent an interesting
challenge to Ben. He'll call on you for help with some background
before he meets with the group. Will that be a problem for your
mathematics course?"
        "Yes, but I'll handle it with Henry Behring as my tutor. See,
I guess I'm learning to give and to receive in my college studies, eh
Professor? The challenge is good for me," Jim stated with a hint of
ambivalency.
        Smith declared, "Good, and as your reward, so to speak, is
an exemption from class attendance and final examinations in theology and ethics. You have to write a term paper for each course.
Figure out what you want to write and clear it with Ben and me."
        Jim mused, "Thanks, I hope I don't disappoint you with my
novice effort at pedantry."
        Professor Smith raised an eyebrow at Jim's choice of words,
teasing him before he walked out the door, "Here's a local Chinook
word for you young man, 'Chechako' means greenhorn, a term
which my colleagues may treat you like, but one no student may do
so. Good luck!"

                                *****

        The wintry days of autumn passed swiftly as Jim followed
the two professors' instructions in teaching theology. He spent as
much time in the library studying and writing term papers. Ben

Adams led him through the faculty lounge often enough that Jim
was considered a teaching assistant amongst the staff. One day
after his world history session, Professor Albertson called him over
to his desk, complimenting him, "James and Ben tell me you're
doing a fine job as their assistant. A real teacher is what they say.
Could you cover my afternoon class tomorrow? You completed
world geography last year as I recall."

"Yes, sir, but I'll have to ask Professor Adams if he can
spare me."

"Oh don't worry, we've got my schedule figured out. Ben
and you can handle it. I want you to administer my world history
test on English monarchs the next day. Perhaps you could discuss
your term paper the latter half of the session. Of course, I'll exempt
you from that test and the final examination. Just finish your three
term papers and you've completed our classes."

By the time Albertson had finished with him, Nancy was
gone and he was late for lunch duty. His singular thought was, *how
can I do all this stuff and run – or visit Nancy?*

*****

Edgar and Esther were married the second Sunday in
December, Jim dazzled by the formal ceremony and multitude of
important guests. He was just as impressed by the posh reception
in the Randall mansion.

Nancy attended with her family and all but ignored the pre-
occupied usher in the borrowed tuxedo. Her brother and his friend
kept her busy, and Jim was so intimidated by the social affair he
stood aside and had dire thoughts about his friend.

*Golly, she should spend some time with me since she's
always complaining that I'm too busy for her. I wonder who that
yahoo is she's smiling at. Maybe I should take Howard's advice
and go over there.*

He greeted Nancy and Jack politely as he approached the
gathering in the corner, polite but not warm responses bothering
him, but he kept his smile in place nonetheless. When Nancy introduced her friends, the name Samuel Gerrity struck a bell – his second den "talks." He exchanged a pleasantry with everyone and
excused himself, a mumbled exchange behind his back producing
a modicum of laughter including Nancy's distinctive titter.

In a snit of anger, jealousy and fatigue, Jim almost left the
reception before the newlyweds escaped to their honeymoon retreat

at the Randall cabin on Vashon Island. He talked to himself all the way home, but nothing deterred his much needed sleep that afternoon and evening. He had another hectic schedule tomorrow.

*****

Professor Smith visited the faculty lounge the next Thursday afternoon and announced his return to his teaching duties. Jim and Ben quickly joined him to return Smith's papers and keys. The teaching assistant found he was a tinge disappointed and realized he had enjoyed his temporary responsibilities.

Jim offered, "If you like, I'll read those term papers nest week, Professor."

"No thanks, Jim. I appreciate the thought, but this old bachelor has all vacation to grade them. I imagine you have lots of work to make up, but I think you should relax. Drop everything and go running with your friends."

Jim smiled and followed his advisor's suggestion, finding a dozen hardy souls braving a light rain as they trotted across campus. As they ran along Yakima Avenue, Mary showed him her engagement ring, Henry grinning ear-to-ear as she stated emphatically, "We're getting married in June, right after Henry graduates. Maybe I can finish up next year."

Henry blurted agreement, "Yes, dear, I'll find a job in Tacoma, and you'll get your degree, too. Jim, remember you promised to be my best man," and when his friend cast him a puzzled look, he added, "Last year you told me to get out of my shell and romance Mary. You said we were made for each other, and then you promised to stand up for me at our wedding."

*****

Jim and the Andersons sailed on the *Dream of Tonstad* to Winslow for the wedding of Howard and Sharon, returning to Tacoma to stand up for Carl when he married Mary before Christmas. He spent the night with Harry Maguire so the newlyweds could have the house to themselves, no honeymoon planned by the older couple.

He found his pockets empty the last day of college classes and was perturbed when Nancy missed their luncheon date. Her absence caused him to worry since she was his most punctual friend, and he trotted over to the Aherne residence after his last class.

Jack opened the door to his rap, inviting him to enter, a warm holiday greeting belied by a piquant face, "Merry Christmas, Jim! Nancy is packing for a visit to Puyallup with Samuel Gerrity. Come into the parlor and say hello to our folks and Sam."

During the next twenty minutes Jim's emotions ran the gamut from impatience to irritation to jealousy as the Ahernes fawned over the Gerrity lad. When Nancy finally appeared, she announced, "I'm ready to leave," and when she spotted him sitting beside her brother, she blushed with an, "Oops! I forgot our date, didn't I?"

Jim grunted his agreement, forcing himself to wish her a happy holiday as he exited as gracefully as he could. Nancy started to talk to his back a couple of times as she showed him out, sensing his anger until she was at a loss for words. He slipped away, trotting back to the University of Puget Sound to attend a faculty party, a social item he had wanted to share with her.

Chapter 9

Hesitating in the entrance to the faculty lounge, Jim was a bit in awe of this social gathering of intellectuals. Ben Adams waved him forward and the Dean's secretary handed him a cup of tea, both accepting his presence as if he belonged here.

"Nice paper, Jim. You've earned your 'A' in my class," Ben stated clearly with a pat on Jim's shoulder.

"Thank you, sir," he replied as a familiar and authoritative voice sounded at his side.

"You deserve it, Mister Gerber. We could use a few more teaching assistants like you. Professor Adams' praise is not lightly earned," announced the Dean.

"And I appreciate his kind words, sir. It's been a tremendous experience for me, and I thank you and my professors for your trust and faith in me," Jim replied, hoping he wasn't overdoing his modesty.

The Dean harrumphed in pleasure, patted his shoulder condescendingly, and remarked, "You're welcome, Jim. Enjoy our little party."

James Smith appeared at Gerber's elbow, both he and Professor Adams chuckling as he complimented his protégé, "Well done Jim, the Dean likes you. Hmm, maybe I should learn to soft soap the boss. You and Ben certainly get results."

Ben laughed aloud while Jim merely smiled, nodding sociably at the Dean as he looked their way. He winked at the two professors as he teased Ben, "Professor Adams is an expert to emulate, sir. All the other staff members think so."

"Ha! Ha! Soft soap and humor each have their place, Mister Gerber. I approve of your attitude. You'll make a fine teacher," Ben said.

"Speaking of teachers, Jim, may I reintroduce Fred Owens from Point Fosdick. I understand you worked for him a couple of years ago," Smith stated.

"Hello, Fred, it's good to see you again. Don't mind my silly remarks, these gentlemen are real teachers. I'm just a helper. What are you doing in Tacoma?"

"Well Jim, I came to see for myself how my former handyman became a student and teacher. Howard swears by you, and these two gentlemen have vouched for you. We need a teacher to replace Howard and want to offer you the position," Fred paused for Jim's reaction.

Professors Smith and Adams nodded, both men aware of Jim's financial straits, and Jim grinned a prompt answer, "Yes, of course, but I'm not a graduate like Howard. Will that be a problem?"

*****

It was a strange feeling standing on the *Kalequah's* deck as a passenger was Jim's amused thought. *I have the urge to work the lines with Ray and Roy or quartermaster for Captain Maguire. Somehow this quiet time is quite different from my hectic schedule of the past few days.*

I was bursting with energy when I called at the Aherne residence to share my news with Nancy, and then completely deflated when I learned she was still in Puyallup the day before Christmas. Howard knew of my appointment, and Esther was staying at her in-laws, so only Carl and Mary could be impressed by my news – not quite what I was looking for.

Well I had a wonderful Christmas at the Andersons, trading gifts and eating and drinking – short as it was. Leave it to Captain Bligh, er Captain Maguire to sail in the middle of the night. I never talked to Nancy or Henry and Mary before I left. I'll write them letters from Point Fosdick after I'm settled.

"Well Jim, are you ready to move into Howard's job? And rooms?" Ray Larsen inquired as he took a well-earned break as the packet plowed up the Narrows.

"You bet, Ray. I'm looking forward to a new experience and regular wages. How are you and Ray doing with the new skipper?"

Ray grunted non-committedly and replied, "We do our work and take our pay, but I miss Rollie and Tellie. You'll see them around the reservation. They're with Hunt at Wollochet Bay and do a lot of work with the tribes. I thought you were going to college."

"Ha! Ha! Going to college and going broke are one and the same to me. I have to pay some loans and put a little money away before summer. I expect Fred Owens will keep me on as a teacher if I do a good job, but I may return to the University next fall," Jim concluded.

"Hmph! Never could figure why anyone needs all that fancy schooling, but Einar swears by it now that he's married to the Widow Barnes with her two children. My brother's on the school board and has turned respectable – hee, hee. Who'd a thought it," Ray chortled.

*****

As Jim stepped onto the dock, a dozen young boys clustered about his legs in greeting, Harry and the older lads grinning happily from a distance. The new teacher recognized most of his students from his stay two years before. As he called them by name ,they beamed at his recognition.

Fred Owens waved the pupils back, ordering, "Boys, remember to show proper respect for your teacher. Harry, why don't you show Mister Gerber his rooms?"

Jim sauntered up the hill behind his young friend, spotting Annie and seven younger girls standing near the school. He returned their shy waves and called them by name as he approached them.

One girl corrected him as he came to a halt, "I'm not Sunny ,Mister Gerber, I'm her sister Sarah. Sunny got married last month and moved to Wollochet Bay."

"But Sunny was…is only…thirteen years of age," Jim puzzled aloud.

Annie understood Jim's confusion and explained, "In our tribe Sunny is old enough for marriage and family life. She turned fourteen in October and is very pretty. Three men came calling on her, and she chose a Squaxin man who works for the Hunt Brothers over at Wollochet."

*****

Jim's popularity as a teacher lasted but a single day, meeting Howard's prediction readily. A school yard fight between two young lads during a game of tag and a sassy response by a fifth-grade girl tested the beginning teacher's control. Jim kept all three students after school for a firm discussion of rules of behavior, the boys cheerful and cooperative but the girl's expression a sullen pout. The teacher walked the girl home and visited with her and her mother until the matter was resolved satisfactorily.

Several minor infractions were handled quickly with punishment by Jim, but he soon realized good behavior resulted from positive reinforcement as well. The second week he placed a clear glass quart jar full of rock candy on his desk, ignoring his students' interest in the object. He shushed the murmur of voices and proceeded the reading lesson, everyone quiet if not attentive. He concluded the exercise by reading a few pages of a story about a seal playing in the harbor and then surprised everyone by asking for a volunteer to read the last page of the story.

He in turn was surprised when his sassy fifth-grader raised her hand, and when called upon she completed the tale without faltering. Looking her in the eye, he smiled and complimented her work, "Well done, Gatchi. Would you like to come up to my desk and choose a piece of candy to chew on while we do our numbers?"

Every eye in the room followed her as she opened the jar and took a piece of pink candy and plopped it in her mouth, giving Jim a mumbled thanks.

"You're welcome. You earned that treat, isn't that right, class?" Jim paused for a chorus of yeses and then continued, "Actually, anyone who does a good deed or gets an A grade deserves a reward. So if you earn a treat, ask me to visit the candy jar. Who cleaned erasers before school this morning?"

One of the third-grade girls shyly raised her hand, and Jim waved her forward to take a candy treat. The class promptly applauded and burst into a ten-minute discussion of "How do I get a candy?"

Before lunch time one of the boys scored a hundred percent on his arithmetic paper and earned a piece of candy: an errant thought popped into Jim's mind, *Here I am bribing my students to be good and study hard. Hmm! Some teacher I am. Ah well, if it works, don't knock it!*

*****

One afternoon during a frustrating arithmetic lesson on the slateboard, Gatchi left her seat to help her little brother add three big numbers together. A murmur of disapproval rippled across the classroom, Jim about to reprimand the girl when an idea came to him.

Ignoring Gatchi's infraction he addressed her little brother,

"Silas, your answer is correct. Tell us how you got it."
The lad laid out his work step by step until he arrived at the answer, inadvertently incriminating his sister, "Gatchi makes it easy."
Jim walked over to the board and wrote down a similar addition problem, and Silas repeated his success by solving the problem. Evidently his sister had succeeded where the teacher failed.
"Gatchi, you did a good job helping your brother. I'm appointing you my assistant for arithmetic, just like Harry is for games during recess. Will you help the younger children while I teach the older pupils multiplication and division?"
Before the end of the week Jim had a tutorial system in place, and even though Fred Owens frowned at the activity during a visit, Jim kept the innovative method in place. He liked the positive growth in the class achievement.

*****

It was always difficult to keep the students focused during a stop, and Jim forgot his academic plans on the packet's visit. He allowed a recess when the boat docked and rang his hand-held school bell after a ten-minute break.
Confident they would respond appropriately, he commenced reading from *The Adventures of Tom Sawyer* even before everyone was seated. Twain's yarn garnered their complete attention.
When three boys looked behind him and shyly pointed to the open door, Jim realized they must have a visitor. He was pleasantly startled to see Nancy, and his reading voice fell away. Everyone was looking her way.
Recovering quickly with a smile and an introduction, he announced, "Class, this lady is my friend Miss Aherne from Tacoma. Gatchi, will you make room for our visitor beside you. I bet if you read the next page, Miss Aherne will read the rest of the chapter to us."
Annie led the discussion of their reading with questions of each student, and everyone participated without any slip. Jim excused the class for a special recess, and shy Silas blurted out the question on everyone's mind, "Is she your girlfriend?"
Nancy laughed and Jim joined her before he finally ordered,

"Silas, go outside...scoot!"

*****

"What a nice surprise! You're a sight for sore eyes, Nancy. How did you escape your father and brother?" Jim paused with a teasing tone when tears glistened in the girl's eyes. "Oh Jim, I have to apologize to you for believing my brother...and my father. Jack told me a twisted story of your den 'talks,' and father sent me to Puyallup to visit my aunt. I didn't even hear about your job here until Henry Behring told me in January. But I didn't hear a word from you either," she concluded with a questioning glance.

Jim grimaced briefly, attesting, "I dropped by your house to share my news, but you were still at your aunt's home. So I posted a letter to you before I sailed to Point Fosdick. I thought you were enamored with Samuel when there was no reply. I was planning on seeing you when I took my final exams, but Professor Smith forwarded my final grades in January – no tests required. I hope you know that I put Ed and Jack on notice that I was serious about courting you...ha! ha!...even if you weren't talking to me. Actually I owe you an apology for being petty and jealous. I should have just told you how I feel about you. I love you!"

"Oh!!!...me too, Jim...I mean I love you, and I ran away from home to tell you. Momma finally confessed the family duplicity, and we had a good cry together. Now I ..."

"Mister Gerber! Mister Gerber! There's a big, mean-looking man looking for you...and her," Gatchi called conspiritually from the doorway.

Nancy's laugh was light but genuine as she replied, "That's my father, Gatchi. Does he have a shotgun in hand?" she joked lightheartedly.

The Nisqually girl was quick, her puzzled look quickly changing to one of collusion as she triumphantly chortled, "Then you are Mister Gerber's girlfriend!"

"You're darned right Gatchi, even if Jim doesn't always admit it. Will you help me? Maybe you and your classmates can show me around the reservation while my men talk."

*****

Nancy's belligerent father stormed through the open door,

muttering incoherently with epithets abounding. Jim continued writing on the slateboard, watching Ed's outraged countenance mutate into bewilderment as his roving eyes searched for his daughter. The transformation allowed the bemused teacher to greet his old friend civilly, "Good afternoon, Ed. Nancy is touring the reservation with my students. Have a seat and we'll talk."

Ed dropped dispiritedly onto a hard bench and stammered, "Where is…I mean…why are…what's happened?"

"Well, Nancy arrived on the *Kalequah* a while back and surprised me with a visit. Oh! I suppose she spent the night on the boat – not to worry, Ed. How did you get here?"

"I sailed to Point Fosdick with a friend in his yawl. Do you realize Nancy ran away yesterday? Hmm, I suppose not if she surprised you. I came to take her home," Ed declared with a fatherly mixture of righteousness and desperation.

Jim smiled to soften his reply, "You shouldn't try to return to Tacoma this late in the day. The Narrows would be tough sailing with an incoming tide and whitecaps roiling its waters. You're welcome to stay with me overnight."

"I won't have my daughter staying anywhere under your influence. I don't want you going near her, you hear, Jim Gerber!"

Jim shook his head slowly and rejoined, "We need to talk…all three of us…I'm still courting Nancy…I hope with your approval."

Harry appeared in the doorway, quietly waiting to be noticed by the two men in their stare-down stance, finally harrumphed a guttural yet polite call.

Jim grinned as he asked, "Yes Harry, where is Nancy?"

"She's spending the night with the Owens family, Mister Gerber. You men are invited for supper at five o'clock. What should I tell her?"

Jim nodded, "Just tell her we'll be there. Her father and I have more talking to do. Thank you, Harry, and give my thanks to Annie and Gatchi as well."

*****

Picking up a lively breeze out of the southwest, the jolly boat scooted around the point and with a favorable outgoing tide disappeared into the Narrows. Jim returned Nancy's wave and stood in place, staring at the rippling surface of Puget Sound.

Oh well, Ed and I got along during supper even though we

argued in the classroom. Missus Owens is a good cook and Fred is a good talker, so the meal went well although Ed made a minor faux pas when he referred to his underaged daughter. But Nancy just smiled and said I was her beau, and she'd be eighteen years of age in the fall. Her father's face darkened with anger, but he was smart enough not to reply.

I'll see Nancy again next month when I have a short vacation. She invited me to a Sunday dinner; I wonder if I have to endure another chat in Ed's den. I can visit the University and check on my standing. Nancy thinks I should return to school, and I agree. I've paid Carl for the loan, and I'll put a few dollars in my bank account while I'm in Tacoma. I just need to find a good summer job.

Ha! Ha! Ed's face was a sight when Nancy kissed me goodbye on the dock. He'd stuck close to his daughter all morning so we couldn't talk privately. Hmph! I'm too slow to romance my girl with Dad in my face. But I did make sure I shook his hand before they boarded the boat, particularly after my fanciful grin at Nancy's precocious and loving behavior. As always my sweetheart is straight forward – more daring than I.

"Mister Gerber! Mister Gerber! It's time for class. All of us want to hear more about your girlfriend and her ferocious father," Harry teased in ribald humor.

Chapter 10

On a Saturday afternoon early in May Jim and Harry borrowed a skiff and rowed to Fox Island Spit on the incoming tide. They made camp amidst a driftwood haven before going fishing for their supper. Harry netted a score of herring for bait, ran a hook through the small fish and cast the line over the side. The pair trolled the northwest shore of the island for over an hour without a bite.

As a fish struck his line, Harry seized the opportunity, his face sagging in dejection as he pulled the fish up to the skiff. With an expressive shrug of his shoulders, the lad conceded, "So it's a dogfish. There are no salmon in the bay, I guess. What'll it be Jim? Herring or shark?"

Jim's answer was to grasp the small dogfish behind his gills and remove the hook, releasing the lucky fish back into the depths. He grinned as he quipped, "I like fried herring. Forget that dogfish, you're not a good enough cook to make it edible."

The two friends continued joshing each other as Harry rowed back to camp. Jim built a warm fire while Harry spitted four herring on alder branches to toast over the flames, jibing his teacher yet again, "Puyallup style...or White Man's?"

"Ha! Ha! I'm with you, Buddy. Leave the little critters whole for roasting, but don't expect me to eat the head...or the guts."

They shared a pleasant interlude at supper, Jim thankful for Missus Owens' homemade biscuits as well as Harry's delicious treat of herring. They crawled into their blankets early because the outgoing tide would start running before daylight. The exposed sandy beaches would provide an excellent clam digging opportunity just at dawn – a gray morning in all likelihood.

*****

A light drizzle fell on the uncomfortable pair, and a breakfast of steamed clams unsettled in their stomachs as Harry rowed vigorously into the rising tide. Jim grunted in discomfort, suggesting, "Let's visit my friend Rollie in Wollochet Bay. We can dry out, maybe beg a meal and go home on the outgoing tide." Harry complied agreeably as he pulled on his left oar and headed inshore.

"Hello, old friends…been clamming on the spit? I saw you pass by yesterday when I was gathering driftwood," Rollie called out as he skipped down the bank to secure the skiff. He shook hands with each in turn, his hardy grip welcoming them to Wollochet Bay.

"Jim, I see you brought your favorite student with you to man the oars. Good thinking! Harry of the Puyallups, you have grown some since last summer."

"Yes, sir, Captain! And strong enough to go to work if you can use a hand this summer," Harry's voice squeaked a bit in his boldness.

Rollie's voice was sober in response, "I just hired a Squaxin named Manny last week, but summer business usually means another hand or two are hired."

"Say Skipper, Harry beat me to it. I have the same need for a job, so keep me in mind as well. Now tell me all the news. I saw Ray and Roy on the *Kalequah's* last visit to Point Fosdick but didn't have time to talk. And how's Tellie?"

"Everyone's fine, Jim. In fact we heard your girlfriend visited you last week…and her father, too," Rollie said with tongue in cheek and a silent request for a story as they entered his small house.

The hour passed quickly, stories and venison stew consumed simultaneously. When Jim and Harry rose to their feet, Rollie offered, "Let me walk you to your skiff by a different path. I need to check on my boat along the way."

Rollie chattered sporadically as he led them toward the beach, expounding South Sound living until his expression became puzzled and he came to an abrupt halt. "Who's on my boat? I don't…oh it's only Manny. Hmm! Working on Sunday yet. Maybe he'll make a good hand yet. Come along, everything's fine there and you need to get home."

*****

A stranger holding a broom entered the classroom after lunch during Jim's story reading. Handing Gatchi his book, he crossed to the young man and led him by the elbow outside, asking, "What can I do for you?"

"I'm Jones, the handyman. I'm here to clean your classroom. What's wrong?"

Jim smiled to soften his reply, "Thank you, Mister Jones. Can you come by here at four o'clock each day? The room will be empty and you won't interrupt a lesson."

"Uh...four o'clock...I clean Mister Owens' office then," the Indian custodian explained haltingly.

"I'll talk to Fred, and I'm sure he'll approve of the change. Please don't come to clean while my students are working," Jim asserted definitively.

Later in the day Jones swept the room and cleaned the slateboard, reporting that Mister Owens had agreed to the new schedule. Jim nodded with a "Thank you," and promptly forgot the routine.

The following Monday the handyman was outside his room at dismissal time, eyeing the older girls and whispering some nonsense to Gatchi. Jim motioned him over to the door, repeating his previous order, "Four o'clock! I don't want to see you before then."

Gatchi hung back to tell her teacher, "That man is bad, Mister Gerber. Captain Trilby fired Manny for bothering Sunny, and Mister Owens hired him anyway. Is it all right for me to punch him in the nose if he says nasty things to me?"

Grinning at his tough young student, Jim said, "Just tell me what this Jones fellow is doing and I'll handle it, Gatchi."

"Hmph! Everyone on the reservation knows Manny is a worthless bounder even if his uncle is a Squaxin Chief," the girl miaowed with a virile lack of respect for the handyman.

Jim replied, "Your vocabulary is improving young lady. 'Bounder' is a good description, but don't repeat that name to anyone else. Like I said, let me deal with Manny Jones."

Jim visited Fred moments later and was assured his new hiree would behave and do his job.

*****

Annie ran into the classroom the next morning with a torn sleeve and scratched arm, breathless and hysterical, "That Manny, he tried to get me into the woods. I'm scared of him."

Jim leaped to his feet, ordering, "Harry, take over the class and do a spelling bee with our new word list."

Striding out the door, he broke into a trot as soon as he rounded the corner, eyes scanning the area for Manny. He burst into Fred's office startling Missus Berry. "Have you seen Jones?"

caused the lady's eyes to swivel toward Fred's empty office, and then he heard the back door slam.

Guessing correctly that the culprit was fleeing, Jim raced for the path to Wollochet Bay in an attempt to cut off the very speedy Squaxin worker. Manny escaped his pursuer by leaping over the bluff and sliding down the sandy slope on his butt. By the time Jim reached the edge of the shallow cliff, Manny was rowing away, pausing but a moment to gesticulate with a closed fist. Jim didn't respond, merely watched him row out of sight to the northwest.

Returning more slowly to Owens' office, Missus Berry informed him Fred was off the reservation. He told her that Manny Jones was a scoundrel and not to be trusted, nor was he allowed in the school or around his students. The Indian lady looked very doubtful but said not a word to the angry teacher.

*****

One of his younger boys returned from the outhouse with a tale, "That bad man is hiding behind the girl's outhouse, Mister Gerber. He shook his fist at me."

"Harry, watch the class," Jim replied as he slipped out the back door and scurried around a brush-covered knoll with a low crouching profile. He was unseen by Manny until he was thirty feet from his skulking nemesis. By the time the handyman noticed the teacher and decided which way to jump, Jim tackled the terrified Indian.

Ignoring a squeaking, "Please don't hit me!" Jim fisted Manny's shirt front and slapped his face with an open palm. He repeated the punishment with the back of his hand, but the Squaxin was a coward and fell to the ground in a crawling escape to Owens' office. Jim looked around at the audience of children and adults who looked approving.

All except for Missus Berry who slammed the door behind her to protect Manny, and shouted angrily, "You have shamed the family of a Chief, you bully. Go away!"

Jim considered the matter closed as he returned to the classroom, all of his students in their seats quietly doing an arithmetic assignment. Harry grimaced in apprehension as he glanced at his teacher, but Jim turned his back on the class and gave him a conspiratorial wink.

Dismissing his class an hour later, Jim requested Harry's help again, "Will you see the children get home safely?"

*****

The next morning Gatchi ran into the classroom early, breathless as she gasped out, "Manny hit Harry with a wooden stick and drug Annie into the woods. Come Mister Gerber! I'll show you."

Jim wasted no time in following the flagging girl to a bleeding but conscious Harry who pointed northwardly. He ordered Gatchi, "Help Harry, I'll find Annie."

Jim raced into the forest, listening to its sounds and scanning for movement ahead. A slap resounded directionless in the woods, a muffled sob coming from his left as he slowed to make his way through dense underbrush. A flash of red plaid caught his eye as he moved silently forward to a giant cedar.

The Squaxin Manny slapped Annie as she fought his grip, tearing her dress as he threw her to the ground. As the villain bent over his victim Jim saw red, anger consuming him. He strode forward and launched a vicious kick into Jones' crotch, a high-pitched squeal of mixed pain and horror eminating from the hapless culprit.

"Annie, go home!"

Manny whirled in his crippled crouch with a wooden branch in hand. Merciless in his punishment, Jim kicked the man in his ribs and dodging the swinging club, smashed his nose with his right fist. A coward suddenly again, Manny tried to run away but the toe of Jim's shoe propelled him off the path into a bramble of blackberries. His screams caused Jim to pause when his anger became laughter as Manny struggled to extricate himself from the bushes, nose bleeding copiously and face crisscrossed with red scratches. His shirt and trousers were shredded before he crawled to Jim's feet and cried for mercy.

"You get out of Point Fosdick and Wollochet Bay. Go back to Squaxin Island. If I see you around here again, I will smack you for sure. Scram!" Jim shouted in disgust, stamping his foot to hasten the scoundrel's departure.

Jim trotted back to school, stopping at Fred Owens' office to report the crime only to be shooed away by Missus Berry, "Mister Owens will talk to you later. He's very unhappy with your bullying ways."

Jim was puzzled by this lack of concern for Annie and Harry until he entered his classroom. Students were in their seats practicing handwriting, Annie seemingly none the worse for wear although Harry's face was swollen and turning black and blue.

*****

It was near noontime and the pupils were working hard on their numbers in hopes that lunch recess could be longer, when Fred Owens appeared in the doorway. Jim walked over to meet him, saying over his shoulder, "Harry, will you…"

Manny Jones' battered face appeared behind Fred, grinning in protected triumph. Jim didn't hesitate, striding past Fred and swinging his right fist into Manny's damaged nose. The villain's grin disappeared as he fell flat on his back into the muddy schoolyard. Jim leaped after the cursing Squaxin, grasping a handful of long hair and slamming another fist into his face. When Jones fell forward to clinch the teacher's legs, Jim drove his knee into the side of the exposed jaw, broken teeth flying about.

"Stop it, Jim! Stop bullying the boy!" Fred yelled angrily and advanced toward the pair of combatants. Another solid right in the eye set the 'poor boy' on his backside again.

Jim spoke clearly in resounding tones for the benefit of the gathering audience, "Manny Jones, you are a coward and a pervert as well as a disgrace to your family. Now get out of here and stay out before I really get mad."

Fred grabbed Jim's arm, and Manny got to his feet with a block of wood in hand, encouraged by the boss's help. Owens pulled on his arm, and Jim pushed him away, Fred 'accidentally' falling backwards over a crouching Harry.

Seeing Fred on the ground caused Jones to drop his stick and back away, falling on all fours to escape another beating. Jim strode forward to grab his belt in one hand and a hank of hair in the other. To his own amazement and gasps of the onlookers, he lifted the whimpering hulk over his shoulders and walked toward the bluff south of the school.

Fred's commands were ignored as he mercilessly ran the last three steps to the rim and cast the twisting torso into the air. Manny flew head over heels out and down the steep slope, striking on his back as a whoosh of air left his lungs, and slowly slid across the sand to land on a gravelly beach.

"I'm coming, Manny. Every time I see…" Jim shouted until Manny had run out of earshot.

*****

"Jim Gerber, you're fired! Pack up your gear and leave," Fred Owens shouted angrily as he ran after his Squaxin charge.

Jim returned to his classroom forlorn and meditative in thought, not realizing until he sat as his desk that every pupil had followed him inside – quietly going to their benches. Feeling their loyalty and love, his familiar grin returned to his face, and was answered by all the children except Harry. His eyes smiled his happiness, but his face was incapable of expression, being one great bruise borne with stoicism.

"Gatchi, will you finish reading our story book? Harry can be in charge of recess afterwards," Jim said as he settled into his gradebook and reports to parents. He was using plain-ruled paper since there were no forms available, and he wrote a message on each report. He was so engrossed in his project that recess came and went before he looked up, his gradebook completed and a separate letter for each pupil stacked on his desk.

"Thank you, class! Everyone deserves a reward for excellent deportment. Annie will pass my jar around the room," Jim instructed and then waited for the treats to be distributed. When the jar came back to the desk with two rock candies inside, Jim took one and offered Annie the extra piece.

He was solemn when he told the children, "Mister Owens has given us an early summer vacation, so I've been making out a progress report for each of you to take home to parents – everybody passed. You can read them before you leave, and I'll answer any questions you might have. I've enjoyed being your teacher, and I hope you will continue in school next year."

Jim was emotionally exhausted by the time he had hugged and been hugged by every pupil. There were tears in Gatchi's eyes when she stood before Jim, "Good-bye, Mister Gerber! You are the best teacher I ever had. Momma and I are going back to live with Daddy and my other brothers and sisters on the Nisqually River. I hope I can go to school there."

"God bless you, Gatchi! I will miss you. Give your mother my best wishes," Jim answered with moist eyes and a bear hug.

As she left the room only Annie and Harry were left seated side by side on a rear bench. After a few moments of silence, Harry announced, "We leave home for good, Mister Gerber. Will you help us? We want to get married and go to Puyallup tribal lands."

In a stubborn and determined voice Annie asserted, "We are old enough. It's time for us to leave Point Fosdick."

Jim merely nodded agreeably and suggested, "If you help me pack my things, I'll help you do the same. We'll walk over to Wollochet Bay and visit Captain Trilby. He's a wise man and your friend as well."

*****

Working for Captain Trilby and his friends made for a pleasant summer job, Jim thought as he steered around Point Defiance one last time before starting classes at the University of Puget Sound. *Where has the summer gone?*

I'm glad we have a delivery of berries and apples for Brown's Point and those boxes of clay pots for Tacoma. I can visit the newlyweds, Harry and Annie, and pass along Fred Owens' wedding present. He was so apologetic for missing the ceremony when Captain Trilby sailed into the middle of Wollochet Bay and married the two sweethearts. Then he admitted Manny Jones was a scoundrel, who was related to Missus Berry. She covered for the ne'er-do-well pervert when he couldn't hold a job anywhere else.

Fred was decent enough to offer me back my teaching position in the fall. Ha! Ha! He sure seemed relieved when I declined.

Nancy and I saw each other three times this summer when I was in Tacoma. The last time we spent the afternoon in Wright Park, just holding hands as we walked and talked. And I was delighted to hear Samuel from Puyallup was engaged to a "nice girl from Sumner."

Maybe I shouldn't be going to college this fall since I'll be broke after paying tuition. And the University is changing to a four- year program with the new College of Puget Sound out in the north end of Tacoma.

Well, a schedule of English composition, geology, theology, drawing and French should keep me busy – a challenge for sure. Of course, Nancy is enrolled in French and drawing. I forgot to ask whether I'll be painting or drafting designs. Oh well, it'll be…

"Avast, mate! Are you headed for Browns Point or Dash Point?"

Jim grinned at Rollie's jibe, "So I've been promoted to 'mate,' have I? And just the two of us aboard the boat. Careful or your new deckhand will expect like courtesy. Are we picking Tellie up at Browns Point?"

Chapter 11

Trotting down Ninth Street without a herd of fellow students seemed strange to Jim, all his running club friends gone except for Nancy. It was late October, and Puget Sound rain was falling as he recalled his transformation back to a student again.

Hmm! I guess that's why my interest in classes is lagging. That and working for Jack Aherne after school and on Saturday. Regular Sunday dinners with Nancy are worth it, and the Aherne wages pay the Andersons for my room. Golly, Jack is hard to live with. He gives me every dirty job in the warehouse to lord it over me. Actually I love the manual labor. I've been doing it all my life, and it keeps me fit.

My so-called friend is always careful not to cross me since he's heard of my clash with Manny Jones. Ah! What I do to keep peace with Nancy's family – it's trying at times.

Mary and Carl are great friends and good company so they deserve Sunday free of my presence. Of course, I escort Mary to church and home before I visit the Ahernes. I do believe they think of me as a substitute son for Howard. He's busy teaching school in Winslow and learning the business with Harold Helmsen – Sven is retiring next year. And Esther lives in Seattle and only visits on holidays. Well I enjoy being pampered by Mary and Carl, it's been a pleasant fall so far.

My classes have gone well except for geology and French. Earth and rocks don't interest me much, but the professor says I'll pass if I keep working. And French is a difficult language to me, but worse yet, the professor is an arrogant fool. Jaques Paquet thinks he's a lover and tries to charm the girls continuously. He criticized my pronunciation the very first day and told me in front of the class, "Any fool in Trois Rivieres can speak two languages well. Practice, fellow practice!"

He backed off when I confronted him after class and hasn't bothered me since and his insolent manner has disappeared – around me anyway. And he'd better not charm my girl – or else!

"Hey, Jim!" interrupted his reverie and brought him to a stop on Pacific Avenue just south of Fifteenth Street. Jack Aherne promptly confronted the panting runner with a weighty corrugated paper box sealed and bound with light rope.

"Here, my friend! Take Father's birthday present to Mom for wrapping, and then pick up a bundle at Puget Sound Freight on the way back to the warehouse. I'll buy you a beer after work." As usual his patron-nemesis vanquished his euphoric state of mind with an errand and casual hand wave good-bye.

Nancy opened the front door to his knock, rising to tiptoes to give him a quick kiss and a cheerful hello. He tried to lean forward to return the greeting with ardor in his eye, but his girl just laughed at his predicament and called over her shoulder, "Momma, Jim's here with Daddy's birthday gift."

Louise bustled into the foyer brushing flour from her hands on her already dirty apron, eyeing both the box and the flushed young man. "James, you deserve a cup of tea for your good deed. Nancy will show you where to hide Ed's present. Come to the kitchen afterwards, and you can tell me what you think of my homemade bread."

Nancy led her beau into the women's sewing room, opening a closet door and stepping aside. Jim deposited his burden on the floor and covered it with a half-finished throw rug. He stepped back to eye his camouflage work, and Nancy bussed him on the cheek. The light thank you immediately turned into a proper kiss as he cradled her in his arms romantically.

When they separated with flushed faces and a bit breathless, Jim chuckled quietly, "And I have Jack to thank for this interlude. Honey, your brother gave me a wonderful errand to run."

*****

Jaques Paquet was a handsome French-Canadian who seemed a strange mixture of intellect, charm and arrogance for a college professor. Jim had tasted his acid tongue one time, and after he confronted him, won a quantum of respect — at least Paquet left him alone. He was smart and instructed his French class well, even Jim able to achieve a satisfactory level of competency. Charming when he chose to be, Paquet had too high an opinion of his appeal to the girls in Jim's opinion. The "French Lover" was self-delusional when it came to women.

One of Nancy's friends was a beautiful girl, and the professor eyed her amorously during the fall. One December day Paquet asked her to stay after class for a conference. Marsha glanced at Jim with a silent plea for help, and Jim settled back into his seat.

"Monsieur Gerber, did you want to see me?" the Professor asked politely.

Just as respectfully Jim responded, "No, I'll wait for Marsha. We're going to the library to study."

Controlling his irritation with obvious effort under Jim's watchful eyes, Paquet complimented Marsha on her work, handing her a French book to read for extra credit. He sat stolidly at his desk as the two friends walked away.

"Thank you, Jim. That man gives me the creeps. He watches me all the time, and one time as I was last to leave the classroom he patted my posterior. Now he wants me to stay with him after class. Hmph! He thinks he's a lover, but I'm not interested," Marsha complained angrily, adding with a touch of panic, "Let's go to the library. That creep may be watching us."

"Ha! Ha! I agree. Don't antagonize the Professor, and you'll get an A. I'll be lucky to earn a C grade regardless," Jim comforted her easily.

*****

Christmas was ten days away when snow fell on Tacoma, the white landscape reminding Jim of his family farm and the wonderful Christmas holidays when he was a small boy. On his way to French class Professor Smith called to him in the hallway, "Jim, can you come to the faculty room and help the President with his Noel party?"

Jim shrugged away his concern for missing French class as he sipped tea with friendly faculty members. Professor Adams arrived late in the hour, raising his eyebrow at Gerber's presence and commenting over his cup of tea, "I let my class leave early so I could accept the President's invitation. What's your excuse, Jim? Professor Paquet is still lecturing his people, and as I recall you're in his class."

"Yes, sir! I'm playing hooky I guess. I was helping with the party arrangements and couldn't say no to the President's invitation to stay. But I'd better go to class and get my assignment," Jim admitted as he grinned abashedly.

Ben Adams gave him a comradely slap on his back, good-naturedly wishing him a Merry Christmas as they parted.

Jim hurried away, passing fellow French pupils along the route. As he neared the classroom door he heard the soft, crooning voice of Jaques Paquet, seeing the Professor blocking a student from leaving the far corner of the room.

"Let me by, Professor Paquet. Your words and suggestions are an insult," came Nancy's angry voice over the teacher's shoulder.

Jim's temper erupted into immediate action as he hurtled across the room snarling, "Paquet! Back off!"

He seized the startled and cowering scoundrel by his shirt collar and lifted him bodily away from Nancy. Wide-eyed at Jim's savage behavior, his girl pleaded, "Don't hurt him, Jim. He's a shameless cad but not worth the trouble."

Gathering courage at the girl's plea, the Professor tried to assert his authority with an indignant protest, "Unhand me, Gerber. I've done nothing wrong. This girl is…"

Nancy's open hand swept across the villain's nose with a resounding "whack," leaving it swollen with a dribble of blood reaching for his upper lip.

Jim laughed harshly but cooled down somewhat, and seizing Paquet's trouser belt in his left fist he forcible marched the bloody-nosed culprit away. The parade attracted considerable attention which Jim ignored, wrestling his squirming victim into the President's office and parked him rather firmly against the broad desk.

"Sir, I protest. I demand these people be expelled. I …," Paquet began.

"Be quiet, you cad!" Jim silenced the man and then addressed the President, "Jaques Paquet is a worthless twit. He thinks he's a lover with the girls. Today he stepped over any level of decency when he assaulted Nancy Aherne — my girl."

"James, you shouldn't have struck a faculty member regardless of your assertion. What…" the President admonished but was interrupted by Nancy.

She declared, "I hit him, Sir. He insulted me with his oafish behavior. Jim rescued me from his advances."

"That's a lie! I can explain everything."

The President held up his palm pontifically and ordered Jim and Nancy, "You two young people wait in the hall. Jim, close the door behind you."

*****

A graceful snowflake danced in the cool air and fell upon Jim's red nose even as Commencement Bay was touched by a ray of sunlight. It was a beautiful wintry day, and the young lovers joined hands in their stroll along the hilltop overlooking the City of Destiny.

Breaking their conspiratorial silence once away from the University, Nancy speculated half to herself, "Well, so much for justice or whatever. Why should we have to drop French from our schedule because Paquet is in the wrong? That ass should be dismissed."

"Tch! Tch! Such language…and near a good Methodist institution," Jim teased his sweetheart, quickly turning serious as he added, "I imagine Paquet got his due in the President's office, but I agree he should be fired. I'm almost sorry I was so restrained. Maybe I should have tarred and feathered him, or punched him in the nose at least. Oh well, I'd probably end up in jail if I gave that rascal his due."

"Hee! Hee! I can just picture poor Jacques being drummed out of town by my knight in shining armor. Hmph! Actually I almost quit school an hour ago. I was so furious I wanted to punch that lecher in the nose. He is such a supercilious scoundrel. Ugh!"

Jim enfolded Nancy in his arms with loving rapport, dropping his unspoken fancy of meeting Paquet off campus to thump him a time or two. He and Nancy were emotionally supportive of one another and didn't need the likes of a pummeled professor to disturb their serenity.

*****

Christmas Eve supper was very special for the Anderson family. Mary and Carl were about to celebrate their first year of marriage with Howard and Sharon and Esther and Edgar joining them for the turkey (and oysters) meal. Nancy had forsaken the Aherne home to be with Jim at the party.

When the men adjourned to the parlor with their brandy, Carl made a surprise announcement, "Mary and I are moving to Gig Harbor. We've found a house on the waterfront with a fishing boat and dock. I was hoping I could talk you into being my partners Jim. I hear they are looking for a teacher to boot. Are you interested?"

Jim cast a glance at Nancy who was studying his reaction with a surreptitious smile, which said she knew him only too well. He wagged his head in doubt but didn't say no, finally turning to Carl with an appreciative response, "I thank you, my friend. Let me think about it. For now I must escort Nancy home before her menfolk come looking for us. Oh Honey, will you gather our coats while I get something from my room?"

Five minutes later Jim and Nancy wished everyone Merry Christmas and strolled down the dark lane to Yakima Avenue where streetlights illuminated their route.

Nancy eyed her beau quizzically and queried teasingly, "What was that line about my family expecting us so early? And what are you thinking about Carl's offer?"

"I needed to talk to you about our future plans – just you and me. Look, I'm not very happy at college. I feel like it's behind me. Not just that Paquet incident, but I want to get on with my life. I've proven to myself I can learn, but I don't want to spend two more years at Puget Sound," Jim explained thoughtfully, Nancy letting him think aloud without interruption.

Under the street lamps at Ninth Street Jim pulled out a small gift package to show her and continued, "I was going to present you this ring tomorrow – maybe on bended knee. I love you, and I want to marry you. Waiting is terrible. Can we live together now? I can be a stock clerk, a fisherman, a teacher or a sailor, but I want to be with you. If you agree to be my wife, we have to decide our future together. Will you marry me, Darling?"

"Oh yes, Jim. I crossed my fingers when you went to your room. I hoped with all my heart that you would propose tonight. It's been a long time coming," Nancy cried happy tears as she kissed her fiancé.

Jim beamed in blissful relief, breathing a poignant sigh as he responded, "I'm lucky to have a woman who understands me so well. I saw your look when Carl made his offer and reckoned you knew my feelings. I'm tired of just holding hands, Wife-to-be. What should we do?"

They resumed their stroll in contemplative thought as she twisted the simple silver band on her finger. As they approached the well-lit Ahern home, Nancy faced him to answer the primary question, "College is nice but not really important to me. Our marriage is everything. Can I go with you to see about that teaching position in Gig Harbor? We could look for a place to live if they hire you. How does January strike you for a wedding – after college finals? We are finishing the term, aren't we?

"Ha! Ha! Yes we are, Nancy dear. Maybe I'd better ask your father for your hand. Then we can set a date which your mother will try to put off. Are you up to breaking the news right now?"

*****

Jim was heavily dressed to ward off the chill on the Anderson dock as he fished the forenoon away. Morning ice was slow melting off the mud puddles along the lane leading to the village center. The solitary figure slapped his gloved hands together to keep circulation in his fingers as he worked his pole and line for a wayward cod or perch swimming in the harbor waters. *Last night's moonlight and today's hazy sun were a nice change for Puget Sound, but that nip in the air is sharp and more than invigorating.* The groom-to-be meditated as he patiently cast his baited hook another time.

I suppose Nancy and Mary are in the village on a secret mission for our wedding. I wasn't invited to the doings. I'm glad the two women get along so well, but maybe if I paid more attention to their plans, it wouldn't seem so mysterious to me. Carl and Mary did us a big favor when they agreed to chaperone us so the Ahernes wouldn't object to our trip to Gig Harbor.

Hmph! The only difficulty in our engagement so far is waiting. The Aherne family accepted the inevitable on Christmas Eve and welcomed me into their clan. Nancy and I were given a free round-trip to Gig Harbor by Harry Maguire although I paid for the Andersons' passage.

After an hour in the village, I was chosen by the school principal as a fourth-fifth grade teacher for next term. It turned out that Einar Larsen was on the school board and insisted I be hired immediately. In the meantime the women found a small two-room cabin for rent up the hill behind Andersons'. I kept my mouth shut when Nancy declared it "perfect," and just shook my head in wonder when she announced her parents would furnish our house. I do believe she forgot we were sharing decision-making. Ha! Ha! Of course I accepted that job on the spot – but she wanted me to.

After the wedding we will spend two nights in the Tacoma Hotel and then sail on the Kahlequah for Gig Harbor. Well at least my days of sleeping on the Anderson sofa will be over. I can share a bed with my wife in our new home, so 1904 won't be so bad I reckon.

*****

"Yoo hoo! Don't look, Darling, I've been shopping for my wedding," Nancy called from the lane.

Jim kept his eyes on the fishing pole as he teased, "'Our' wedding is only three weeks away so maybe I should peek."

"Shush! Be a dear and go help Carl with our washtub. Treat it carefully since it will serve as our bathtub also. Carl says he can fix the broken stove so it's as good as new. I've saved us a lot of money today."

"Ha! Ha! And spent my first month's salary no doubt," Jim essayed as the door slammed behind him.

He thought silently, *Maybe I should be more serious about my fiancée's shopping before that sofa calls to me again.*

His smile turned nostalgic as the *Kalequah's* horn sounded from the harbor entrance. He hurried to complete his chores. The foursome would be leaving in an hour or so.

Chapter 12

The Larsen brothers waved imperiously to the newlyweds, gesturing them forward to the *Kalequah's* gangplank. Their expression of mischief and excitement was explained by the discordant greeting ringing out from a small crowd on the Gig Harbor dock. Giant Einar Larsen and his cronies were flanked by a smattering of townfolk and Principal Samuel Conrad and several children – his clan of students, Jim reckoned correctly.

"Oh my!" murmured a somewhat abashed bride, and Jim laughed at her reaction as he waved gaily in return.

Ray Larsen promised, "Roy and I will see all your furniture gets ashore, Jim. Our brother and his friends will deliver it to your house right away. Best wishes!"

"And God bless you," Roy added shyly, his usual roughhouse appearance tempered by Nancy's presence. He murmured a thought being expressed by several voices near the gangplank, "You're sure lucky, Jim."

A tinkling laugh escaped Nancy's lips with a pretend-poke in the ribs and teasing words, "See, my brother's right after all."

"You mean about my marrying above my station in life. I never disagreed with Jack, did I?" Jim concurred as he shook hands with his volunteer moving crew, not offended by the resounding slaps on his back.

Nodding to Mister Conrad, he asked the pupils gathered around the Principal, "Did you all come to say hello to your new teacher?"

A chorus of "Yes, sir!" echoed through the damp air of Gig Harbor, and Sam Conrad laughed aloud, his endorsement of Mister Gerber following, "Welcome! These youngsters have been waiting for relief from the Principal teaching the class. Can you start tomorrow, Mister Gerber?"

Glancing around at the expectant faces produced a grin and acceptance of his responsibility, "Of course! I'll see you all in the morning."

*****

116   Royal LaPlante

"Twenty-one, twenty-two and twenty-three," Jim counted each step until he stood on the railed stoop before their cabin. "I see Carl replaced three planks in the stairway," he announced to his wife.

"It's just fine, Dear. Maybe you should build a railing up here so we don't fall down the hill on a dark night," Nancy replied, casting a critical eye over the steep hillside.

Jim's response was to pick up his bride and carry her over the threshold, oblivious to Einar and his grinning crew. The men actually chuckled when he kissed her in the front room of their new home.

"Ahem!" Einar interrupted. "Where do you want your bed?...Leo, put that stove against the wall here and help Lars install it. Well Jim?"

"Go to it Einar. The back room is our bedroom with the headboard to the north and that dresser under the window. Is the floor stout enough for that heavy iron range and some cordwood?" Jim pondered aloud.

Einar nodded with surety, "The old fellow who built it used eight-by –eight cedar piling. But I don't know about this hillside – will it slide?"

Leo spoke up from the stove, "Heinz lived here for years without any slide, but I bet he froze his butt off. I feel a draft even when the door is closed."

"My wife is going to remove the old newspaper covering the wallboards and paste real wallpaper over it. The cedar shingles will keep the rain out, and maybe the new paper will stop the wind. Laying a fire in that fine range is our first job," Jim urged his two volunteers.

Lars soberly promised, "In ten minutes, Jim." The blacksmith was molding the stovepipe into the roof fitting as his partner braced the middle of the chimney out from the wall.

Meanwhile Nancy had two older men scraping the sodden newspapers from the far wall, her gregarious nature charming all of Einar's work gang. Jim stepped outside to check the outhouse, finding the open trench under the stool very shallow. At his elbow Larsen suggested, "Maybe we should dig a new hole on the other side of the cabin. This one's not very good."

Jim grimaced at Einar's understatement as he retorted, "It's full up and stinks, you mean. Yes, I'll dig a deep hole after school tomorrow. Do I have my priorities right, my friend? The stove first, followed by the bed and then the outhouse."

"Some honeymooner you are – the bed second? Well, we'll take your outhouse apart and put it back together over your new hole. Three o'clock tomorrow?"

*****

"Mister Gerber," no backtalk, studying quietly at desks, all caused Jim to ponder his students' behavior as he leaned back in his chair awaiting Samuel Conrad's visit. *Golly, these youngsters are just too nice. Why did my predecessor abandon his classroom before Christmas? Einar's friends regaled me with tales of mischievous, misbehaved and mistaught children lurking in my classroom. It seemed only the Principal could handle this wild bunch. Hmph! Probably giving me a day of calm before trying their shenanigans. Oh well, today was fun. I better enjoy it while it lasts. I wonder why Sam asked to meet with me after school. I haven't had time to...*
"Thanks for staying Jim. How did your day go?" the Principal interrupted Jim's thoughts and joined his peaceful melancholy as he perched on the nearest bench.
"Fine Sam, although they were awfully well-behaved for their reputation. When should I expect the revolution – any suggestions?"
Conrad chuckled and grinned as he replied, "I anticipated a half-dozen boys would test you today. That's why I asked you to confer with me after school. When everything went so well, I decided to visit with your eldest pupil during afternoon recess and sure enough Caleb told me your secret power. The boy's grandmother is a Puyallup and he's kin to Harry of Browns Point. You are Harry's hero as well as friend, and Caleb told that Point Fosdick story to his classmates. Fred Owens had told me of Manny Jones when he recommended you as a 'great' teacher. Evidently your pupils are impressed."
"Ha! Ha! I hope they aren't so scared of me they can't learn. I like creative thinkers as well as dependable children."

*****

The alternate patterns of school with children and weekends fishing off Point Defiance became more tolerable as spring freshets arrived in March. Jim became familiar with the swirling eddies of the deep waters off the Point, and fished there alone when the Andersons spent the Easter holiday in their Tacoma home.

Nancy liked to be busy, substituting for sick teachers after fixing up their cabin. She pestered her husband until he agreed to take her along on his boat on Good Monday. The two newlyweds enjoyed an active day on the choppy waters off Point Defiance and around the bend into the Narrows. When Nancy hooked one last Chinook to add to their catch, they found a thirty-plus pounder with a will of its own. Nancy was determined,however, and after a half-hour won the battle. She was ecstatic when Jim gaffed the huge fish and hauled it over the side of the boat.

Neither had noticed their position in the Narrows nor the tidal flow. They discovered they were halfway down the channel opposite Point Evans, and the incoming tide was carrying them faster than they could row. With daylight fading under a cloudy sky, Jim proposed an overnight camp, "Honey, I can clean the salmon on the beach. We can return to Gig Harbor in the morning and deliver our fish to the buyer. Hey, we can eat the smallest salmon and what's left of your homemade bread for our supper."

"And share a night under the stars...oops...under the clouds I guess. It'll be an adventure to remember. Where do we camp, Husband?"

Jim chuckled and pointed to the near shore, "On the Tacoma side where I spent a night one time. It's sandy and comfy, but watch out for the poison oak."

"Ugh! I'm itchy just at the mention of that weed. You can round up driftwood for a fire while I clean a salmon for our meal," Nancy decided as their boat found an eddy which reversed their direction.

Jim nodded as he leaned on the oars until the boat wavered in the tidal ripple, and then he rowed sixty feet into shore to their campsite.

*****

Having a Saturday off was invigorating to the teacher-fisherman as he perched on the edge of his stoop and leaned against the railing. Jim basked in morning sun and dreamed of more pleasant nights and warm sunny days. *I bet Nancy thinks her "perfect" home has materialized with the spring weather. Of course I always agree she's a terrific homemaker.*

My wife was determined during the winter to transform the cabin into a real home and she succeeded very well. The front room walls are covered with tasteful and durable wallpaper, golden hues brightening our front room and pastel green overlaying the bedroom.

I don't know how she finds just the right color and pictures to uplift our spirits, but she does. That framed daguerreotype of Old Tacoma and its lumber mills was a real find. It hangs next to the iron range on the south wall, and on the opposite wall are a pair of pastel paintings picturing early Gig Harbor. Finally there is that rather imperfect drawing of a Chinook salmon by Caleb which is pinned to the felt board by the door, along with a tidal calendar and my bright red ribbon from the fishing derby last month.

I bought a simple fir table with two chairs for the corner by the window, and Nancy's folks gave up a drab brown love seat set against the bedroom wall. Then Louise gave me a venerable old teak rocking chair her father had left her – a family heirloom no less. Jim thought for a moment and chuckled, but I love it for evening relaxation.

Nancy's cedar chest sits in the corner with a wicker basket atop, and a small corner shelf has a display of seashells from Day Island and clay babies from Fox Island. Frilly curtains on the two windows in the front room and heavier drapes over the bedroom windows somehow make my wife's work other than utilitarian.

"What time is the ballgame? Do you have time to go to the general store with me?" Nancy asked from the open doorway.

"Yes Ma'am! My umpiring duties don't start until eleven o'clock. It'll be fun calling balls and strikes between my old class at Point Fosdick and my new school team. Carl's coming along to keep me company since we're not fishing today. Later maybe we could visit with Carl and Mary about fishing fulltime. Sam asked me if I was going to return in the fall and I need to answer him Monday," Jim related with a quizzical look for Nancy's consideration.

His wife gave her supportive answer, "You make more money fishing than teaching. We've paid off all our bills with both jobs so you can do what you want. Which is fishing I expect."

*****

Jim bought a flat-bottom small skiff with his last teacher's pay. Working both boats off Point Defiance increased the partners' income significantly, and Nancy could go along to camp overnight at their favorite spot on the Narrows.

One day in August the couple came upon an old man towing a raft of scrap lumber up the waterway, evidently headed for their campsite. Unfortunately, the outgoing tide had turned and the fellow was in trouble. Jim rowed near to the fishing boat and cast a short line to the struggling oarsman, who quickly attached it to his bow ring while missing only a couple of beats. Two men rowed in consonance and the raft maintained its progress even as the currents quickened.

An hour later they nudged the gravel beach and sighed loudly, Nancy and Jim dragging their skiff high and dry, and then repeated the action with the second boat. Jim went back to the water's edge to help the stranger, commenting thoughtfully, "Do you want to tote this lumber above the high water mark? There's usually an evening breeze before sunset. Could break up your raft."

The old fellow turned to face Jim with a knowing smile, "Jim Gerber, isn't that your name? We met on this spot a couple of seasons ago if my memory is sound."

Jim grinned in agreement as he recalled, "Ling cod cheeks are good but liver is inedible, Oscar. I remember your hospitality but not your last name."

"Miller's the name, and no relation to that fellow that claimed this land. You a married man now?"

Nodding happily Jim acknowledged, "With that lovely lady up there. Wave to Nancy and she'll feed you a fine meal after we carry your lumber to the hillside. Are you going to build a cabin here?"

"Yup! Big Oscar's Camp is what I'll call it. Maybe I ought to name this beach something other than the Narrows. Oh well, I'll talk to the fishermen who are building next to me. You and your Missus are welcome to stay here anytime, Jim. I'll tell 'Mad Phil' about you. He plans to live here year around and thinks we should have rules like up in the Klondike gold camps."

Overhearing the men's conversation as they toted lumber high and dry, Nancy quipped, "Of course, salmon are as good as gold around here. Hurry up Gentlemen, dinner is about to be served."

*****

Jim eased into the overstuffed chair and sipped his brandy as his father-in-law "instructed" him on Tacoma affairs. The young couple was spending the Christmas holidays with the Aherne family, actually in Nancy's old room. Church and Christmas dinner behind them, another session in the infamous den was in progress. Ed and Jack now accepted Jim as a family member and wanted him to move to "civilization" and join the business.

Ed postulated an attractive offer intended to convince his son-in-law to accept, "You'll be floor boss for a year or two and I'll teach you the business at the same time. When Jack steps up to Vice-President you can move into his manager's job. Louise has even found a nice house down the street where you and Nancy can live. We'll help you purchase it if you'll let us."

Jim smiled warmly but subtly stalled the conversation, "I'll discuss it with my wife later. Now tell me more about the City of Destiny – and our grand state. Gig Harbor never seems to hear the news."

Jack responded affably, "Our Alma Mater is now a four-year college, and moving to a permanent campus in the north end of town. And your friend Captain Roland Trilby returned to the Kalequah as skipper just this week."

Ed interrupted eagerly, "Rollie got a nice raise and the fancy title of First Captain. Why don't you join me tomorrow and we'll buy him a drink. Jack has to watch the warehouse."

"Sure Dad, and do give your friend my best regards," Jack agreed as he added, "I saw that Puyallup friend of yours during the summer, what's his name…"

"You mean Harry at Brown's Point?"

"Yah, he was working to clean up the grounds around the new lighthouse. It started operation about the same time as the Pavilion out at Point Defiance Park. Visitors will ride the streetcar out there one of these days," Jack declared.

Jim nodded but his question changed the subject, "How's Foss Tug doing? I see a lot of their boats moving log rafts around the sound."

The elder Aherne replied, "I talked to Andrew not too long ago and he sounded like a real business tycoon, but I still think Thea runs everything."

Jim chuckled as he quipped, "Behind every successful man is a good woman. Applies to me as well Ed. You raised a fine daughter."

The men nodded in unison before Jack continued the news report, "A rumor says the Guggenheim brothers are going to buy out the smelter if Old Man Rust agrees. Progress I guess. Say Jim, is Carl going to buy one of those new outboard motors for his boat? More fishing and less rowing makes sense to me."

Ed grinned conspiritually at his son as he commented, "Of course you needn't worry about such business if you'll join us. Take my offer. Carl and Mary will probably move back to Tacoma."

Jim merely smiled enigmatically as he sipped his brandy, enjoying the Aherne den for the first time.

*****

Nancy beamed with pleasure when Jim and Ed returned home the next day and her husband announced that Rollie had hired him for a couple of trips while the Larsen brothers vacationed in California.

Jim quipped, "Honey, you don't have to look so pleased that I'll be gone for a few days. Visiting your family seems to agree with you, just like Mary and Carl staying over at their Tacoma home for the winter. I'll batten up both houses when we stop at Gig Harbor later in the week."

Louisa and her daughter exchanged cheerful hugs and Ed grinned happily as well, even as Nancy jibed, "Don't look so self-satisfied Daddy. It'll be a lovely vacation but we're returning to Gig Harbor afterward. My husband and I appreciate your support and your job offer, but we love our life over there. Fishing is what we both want to do."

Jim breathed a sigh of relief at his wife's support in breaking the news to her parents. They accepted her position with a nod and even smiled at their son-in-law. It seemed that all was well in the family.

Chapter 13

Swirling masses of dismal rainclouds shrouded the *Kalequah* as she left Olympia, visibility a neglible problem for Jim as he steered a mid-channel course through the South Sound. A squall line crossed over the packet, splattering large raindrops against the wheelhouse windows as the Captain signaled the quartermaster to starboard and a southeast heading. Moments later a shaft of sunlight pierced the pall to port and revealed Anderson Island, following behind the squall towards Dupont, and then gone moments later.

Jim squinted into the haze and asked, "Skipper, can you give me a heading on Anderson Island's south point? I figure we're a mile from our northerly turn. I don't want to end up on the Nisqually Flats."

"You're on the mark, Jim. Stay on this course for five minutes and maybe the rain will let up," Rollie suggested and added a wistful thought, "I wish you'd stay aboard for another trip. I don't know if the Larsen brothers are back yet."

Jim grinned but declined, "I miss my wife, Rollie. These three weeks with you have been fun, but I'm a married man. Besides, I worry about Nancy being spoiled in her father's home. It's too nice and comfortable. We can only afford cabin living unless I go to work for my father-in-law. Ugh!"

"I know how you feel, and I agree that a clerking job with 'Daddy' isn't good for you younguns. Hey look! The mist is clearing ahead. There's the Nisqually valley. Bring our lady to a new heading for Dupont," Rollie ordered serenely.

The *Kalequah's* bow touched the wall of everchanging clouds of mist once more as she sailed toward their next stop, Rollie suddenly snapping erect to shout, "My God! What's that...?" and sounded the boat's horn repeatedly.

Jim acted spontaneously, ringing the engine room for full astern as he spun the wheel hard astarboard, feeling but a hint of a shudder as timbers crunched loudly in the moist air. Blurry voices shouted tinnily beside the *Kalequah*, words indistinguishable but understood nevertheless.

"Stopping all engines!" Jim shouted to the Captain as he hurtled his body into the stairway. A fishing boat with four men,

Nisquallies in all likelihood, had materialized from the fog at just the wrong moment and lay shattered beside the bow. The quarter-master stood at his post until it was clear Tellie had acted and then bounded down the stairs to follow Rollie to the open cargo door on the port side. The young man filling in as a deckhand emerged from the galley and stood confused on the cargo deck.

Jim ordered brusquely, "Life rings, Johnny. We've struck a fishing boat."

Rollie already had a doughnut-shaped cork lifesaver in each hand and cast them into the sound, both rings grabbed by three fishermen before Jim reached the side. Surveying the tragic scene with an eye for detail, Jim shed his heavy sweater in a nonce and then kicked off his moccasins. Following the three Indians' gestures of distress, he spotted the bobbing head of the fourth Nisqually drifting away from the boat.

Rollie frantically cried, "He's a bloody mess, Jim. I don't think he can see us. Look! He's stroking away toward the west – really confused."

Jim yelled, "I see him, Skipper," and hopped atop the *Kalequah's* bumpers to run astern, no real deck to support his feet. Slipping, he managed to jump clear of the hull. Swimming vigorously to the surface, Jim put all his youth and strength into his stroke until the man's head was lost from sight.

He heard much-needed encouragement from Rollie and his best guess, "You're doing fine, Jim. Go ten feet ahead and dive deep for that lad."

Automatically following the Captain's calculations, he took four long strokes and gulped a large breath of salty air before diving below the surface. The water was as gray as above the surface and got dimmer still as he descended. His stockinged left foot became entangled with the thrashing form of a drowning man. Jim grabbed a handful of waving long hair in his fist and struck out for the surface.

Fresh air never felt so good was his irrelevant thought as the berserk Nisqually frantically tried to climb atop his rescuer's head. Fortunately, Johnny threw a lifesaver right on target, and both men were saved from fighting each other. In a few moments they were hauled aboard by the crew and the other survivors.

Jim raced shoeless and breathless up the cold steel treads to the wheelhouse to call for power and steer for shore, Rollie soon beside him to take the wheel and praise the tired young man,

"Thanks, Jim. You saved that lad's life just now. We'll meet that Nisqually canoe coming out of the river and transfer the survivors. We can report the incident to the authorities in Tacoma. Thank God no one was lost," Rollie concluded as he reversed engines and came about to meet not one, but three canoes waiting nearby.

At Rollie's nod Jim descended the stairs, retrieving his moccasins before escorting the four Nisqually men to the starboard cargo door. A tribal elder in the lead canoe silently appraised his kinsmen, and with a satisfied nod waved the eldest survivor into his canoe, the two uninjured men boarding the second canoe.

The battered lad awaited the third canoe while the elder shouted toward the wheelhouse, "Captain Trilby! You owe me a fishing boat – a good one."

"Yes, old friend, and a five dollar gold piece as well. Jim will fetch it for you," Rollie replied willingly.

Jim was quick to transfer the Skipper's coin to the Elder, even as the fourth survivor was greeted warmly by his young wife.

"Mister Gerber! Thank you for saving my husband. You are our friend forever," shouted a young woman whose voice was so familiar that Jim recognized her as Gatchi from his Point Fosdick class.

His immediate thought was that the girl had become a fetching woman very quickly, and remembering he was an "old" married man, Jim responded as his teacher of yore, "You're welcome, Gatchi. You've got a good man there. Take care of him, old friend."

*****

A week later the teacher found himself before his old class of students at Gig Harbor, recalling his satisfaction in seeing a mature Gatchi, a happy Harry and pregnant Annie at Browns Point, and Sunny with her husband and two children at Wollochet Bay. Teaching was filled with satisfaction so he jumped at the chance to fill in the month of February, and Sam Conrad was elated to have a 'tough' substitute on duty. Smiling at his emotions, he concluded that he'd no doubt have enough of the active classroom before the regular teacher returned from Seattle.

Weekends in Oscar's cabin at the Narrows were almost a vacation for the young couple, Carl's bigger boat a much-appreciated bonus when the Andersons stayed in Tacoma during the winter. Nancy and Jim enjoyed the best of both worlds.

The last Saturday of February Jim was fishing the incoming tide off Point Defiance. Carl was still in Tacoma and Nancy was baking today, so he was enjoying his solitude. He had just caught his supper by fishing the bottom – no salmon but a pair of red snappers graced his fish box. His southerly drift into the Narrows brought him within sight of Oscar's camp and an unusual bustle of activity before it. He hauled in his gear and rowed vigorously to the Narrows to see what Oscar was doing.

Several old-timers greeted him warmly as he beached his boat, helping him secure it before handing him a shovel and a job, "Dig deep, Jim, we have to set three more pilings before the high water reaches us."

Oscar explained further, "Got a real deal on these two rafts of pilings from a fellow at Titlow Beach. You know how the waves lap at our floor on a high tide and a windy day. Well eight-by-eights don't do the job, so I'm putting in twenty strong pilings and raising my clearance by two feet."

"Yah, and we'll plank over the front end to keep driftwood from under the cabin," his neighbor drawled, grinning in pleasure when Jim nodded in enthusiastic agreement. It seemed the Narrows was getting to be a permanent camp.

Before Jim left on the outgoing tide, he had become part of Oscar's work schedule. After all, he thought as he waved good-bye, *I'm going to use this cabin for weekend fishing. Hmm, maybe I'll build a place for myself.*

*****

Carl's face was pale in the bright sunlight, but he coughed again and then again. Seeing the pain in his friend's eyes, Jim declared in a tone which brooked no dissent, "We're going in, partner. You're in no shape to fish today."

Shaking his head in frowning negation, the older man choked in a paroxysm of coughing, spitting phlegm over the side as he gasped for breath. Jim rowed hard to reach Gig Harbor in the next hour, and of course Carl didn't cough at all, seemingly without a breathing problem.

"All this worry is for naught, Jim. I'll be fine tomorrow. That fancy doctor called it pneumonia back in January, but I'm over the sickness. I can still fish," Carl asserted, trying very hard to convince himself as well as his partner.

Anderson's persistent ailment lasted for months and frustrated the partners' fishing. By late June he appeared hale and hearty, and their salmon harvest was bountiful through the summer. One day in mid-August Carl collapsed in another bout of lung fever, this time diagnosed as pleurisy. Mary decided her husband's fishing career was over with a tearful announcement to Nancy and Jim, "The doctor says Carl's lungs are damaged, and he needs to stay off the Sound – no fishing. We're selling our Gig Harbor house and moving back to Wright Park full-time. Besides he's sixty-four, and we don't need the money. He says the boat's yours to keep. 'Good fishing' is his wish."

*****

The ensuing weeks were prosperous for the Gerbers, their shanty in Gig Harbor always pleasant in the sunny days of summer. Added to their bliss was Nancy's announcement that she was with child, actually expecting in late January. As men will do, Jim celebrated by buying a five-horse outboard motor fitted to Carl's fishing boat.

He confirmed his wish that their baby be born in Tacoma at her folk's home, even conceding, "Maybe I can work for your Dad this winter while Jack is visiting his lady love in Salt Lake City. I'd feel better if we paid our room and board."

Nancy just laughed at the latter remark, "Mother invited us to stay long ago. Both of my parents will enjoy being grandparents. Ha! Ha! Maybe they should pay us for the privilege. Besides Dad will really appreciate your help."

"How did Jack ever connect with a Mormon lady from Utah?"

Nancy shrugged her shoulders and guessed, "Laura Young is pretty and nice as well. As you said, she's a lady. He was introduced to her at the Church of Latter Day Saints downtown when he was meeting a friend. You know, I think he's going to ask her to marry him. We don't know what her family thinks of this romance. Her religion doesn't pose any problem for us Ahernes, but what about her parents?"

These two topics of conversation occupied a great deal of their thoughts as autumn leaves began to show their changing color. The couple frequented Oscar's cabin on fishing trips whenever their friend was away and the beautiful weather lasted.

In late October they crossed over the Sound to the small settlement on the Narrows, every fishing camp closed up except for Oscar's. His boat was tied to the slip and banging gently against a nearby piling as they neared the beach. Sensing a problem, Jim drove his bow right at the ship's winch and shouted, "Tie our boat to the pulley, Dear. Something is amiss. Where's Oscar?"

He cut the motor and tilted its propeller out of the water before leaping over the side to the landing, hurrying through the gaping doorway of the cabin and shouting his friend's name. A muffled reply of pain came from the front room, and Jim discovered his friend lying near the cold woodstove, an aroma of sweet putrid flesh assaulting his senses. Oscar's right hand was torn by a hook and swollen, a tinge of blue at the wrist. His fingers were cut as well, and Jim surmised blood-poisoning was at work below a belt tourniquet midway up his lower arm. Oscar needed medical attention for such a serious infection.

Hearing Nancy choking back her bile at the horrible sight, he hesitated until she ordered, "Release the belt while I slice his hand and drain the poison. He needs to bleed freely for a few seconds before we carry him to the boat."

Puss and blood oozed from the swollen hand before Jim tightened the belt again and unceremoniously cradled the limp body in his arms to carry him to the boat. Nancy followed, untying the rope and pushing off when the old man was safely sprawled in the bottom of the boat. She sat down beside him and held his head in her lap as Jim cranked his outboard into life. A race against time followed, the turning tide saving precious moments as they hastened to Rust's Smelter.

As a result of their quick actions and Nancy's first aid, the doctor was able to save part of Oscar's hand, three middle fingers falling victim to fish poisoning.

Felix Miller sailed down from Ballard to take his brother home to Seattle. He stopped at Gig Harbor after picking up Oscar's camp gear and boat, announcing, "The doctor praised your first aid at the camp. Claimed it saved Oscar's hand if not his life. My brother is going to be an invalid for a long while, and he's not too young either. He wants to sell you his cabin for a hundred dollars. Are you interested?"

"Yes, of course, Felix. Would it be all right to stop by his sickbed tomorrow with the money? We'd like to visit with Oscar as well as pay him," Jim replied quickly.

*****

Rollie Trilby and his crew volunteered to move the Gerber household from Gig Harbor to the Narrows after the couple decided to give up their hillside shack and move to the fishing camp – their new home. Nancy carefully transferred curtains, pictures and throw rugs to their Narrows cabin while the *Kalequah* delivered their furniture. She even baked a batch of sugar cookies and treated their friends to coffee and sweets before the boat continued on its rounds.

Jim chuckled at Rollie's nervousness as they waved goodbye to the *Kalequah* and its crew, suggesting, "The Skipper was torn between your company and cookies, and the outgoing tide. He only had a fathom or so of water under his keel when we ferried the furniture to our slip."

"Oh, I thought he was worried about the kelp bed out there. Can't it foul up his propeller?"

"No, not with the *Kalequah's* power, but our outboard is another matter. I sheared a pin last month when my propeller cut into that seaweed. Now let's put our house in order. We can clean up the Gig Harbor cabin when we go to stay with your folks next week," Jim concluded.

The new owner happily tarred a few spots on his roof, a task Oscar had remembered to describe for him, and then finished chopping a load of cordwood for their iron range. Finally he leaned his skiff on its side behind the house, and helped his wife move the furniture around, hopefully for the last time. When they ran out of all their food, except flour and fish, the couple headed to Gig Harbor to sell fish before heading for Tacoma. Nancy's time was but a few weeks away, and Christmas was not far off. It was time to visit the Ahernes and live the city life for a couple of months.

Chapter 14

Jim leaned back in Ed's office chair, eyeing his minions as he pondered to himself, *I laughed when my father-in-law asked me to stand in for him. He even left me a couple of bow ties to wear at work. Ugh! And the new year started out so satisfyingly unpretentious.*

Jack left for Salt Lake City on a Northern Pacific train just before Christmas, and I enjoyed the work in the warehouse while the doctor was pronouncing Nancy hale and hearty on every visit to his office.

I saw the Andersons over the holidays, along with Howard and Sharon, and Esther and Edgar. The young wives both shared their news with us that they are expecting. Howard told us he quit teaching and is a partner in the Helmsen store, and Edgar smugly announced he is a cashier in his father's bank.

Nancy and I visited Professor Smith the Sunday afternoon before Christmas, and he gave us a newsy report on the College of Puget Sound. He was aglow with praise for the new campus, albeit any permanent buildings. Maybe we should have ventured to the college's new site at Sixth and Sprague, but Nancy tires easily these days. It seems to me my wife can do anything she wants, but not on the same day. Rest is part of her "expecting" status.

Henry and Mary Behring came to supper at the Ahernes one evening, both old friends looking well enough but appearing a little blue to Nancy. My wife discovered the cause, Mary miscarried in November, but she and Henry are determined to try again next year. I think Henry was a bit jealous, well envious anyway. He asked a lot of questions about Nancy's health and our plans for the baby.

And then that infernal telegram arrived at the house inviting the Ahernes to visit the Youngs in January. Darned if they didn't pack up and leave for Utah the following week. Here I am sitting in Ed's office and looking important – or trying to anyhow. Hmph! Everyone humors me as Straw Boss even though they all know I turn to Aunt Edith before I make any decision. Heck, it was more fun unloading freight or filling orders than wearing a collar and tie. I like to use my hands.

"Mister Gerber!" broke into his thoughts, a middle-aged Floor Manager named Josh something-or-other claiming his attention.

"Yes, Josh…"

"Sir, the Seattle order is almost ready. You know, that large one you were working on last week. But we're missing three bolts of cloth," Josh explained.

"And can't we send the shipment without those bolts?"

"Yes, sir, but Edith suggested I go down to the Tacoma Mercantile and buy them so we send a complete order. Is that all right?" the flushed employed inquired.

"Of course, Josh, see Mister Hastings for the cash and do as Edith suggests. Good work!" Jim praised his boss-of-yesterday.

As the man hurried away on his errand Jim chuckled, a laugh or two escaping his lips. His eyes flicked to and fro to see if anyone had heard his guffaw. Well, so much for "major" decisions. If Aunt Edith holds her own, I guess I'm doing my job. I hope Ed gets back here sooner rather than later.

*****

An announcement of the Young-Aherne engagement arrived by mail the day before all three Ahernes returned home. Jack was uncharacteristically positive and chatty as soon as he walked through the doorway. He even acceded to Jim's expertise as a "married man," and asked for advice on planning for his big wedding in Salt Lake City.

"Ha! Ha! Jack, slow down! First of all your fiancée and her mother will do all the planning, not you. Ed, didn't you tell your lovestruck son that his women make all these kinds of decisions?" Jim teased his flustered brother-in-law.

Ed nodded sagely, claiming, "I told him, but he's a bit deaf at the moment, I guess."

"Ah Dad, I heard you, but Laura said I could help. Oh…you mean if she asks me. Is it always like this, Jim?" Jack queried tentatively.

"Now you're listening, Jack. Tell us about your trip and more about Laura and her family."

"Ah, trains are boring, but seeing Salt Lake City with Laura was an adventure. The Youngs live downtown between the Mormon Temple and the railroad depot. We could walk everywhere it seemed, except for our trip out to the Great Salt Lake. Mister Young drove his family carriage out there for a picnic. Laura has two brothers and five sisters who are younger than she is, so it was quite a crowd. Everyone went swimming in the lake, which was a new experience for me. I couldn't sink in that salt water."

"Is it true that Mormon men have more than one wife? Does her father?" Jim asked quizzically.

"Yes, polygamy is common enough with the old-timers. I didn't ask Laura that question in regards to her family. They didn't talk about such subjects when I was around, and I didn't stick my nose into Mister Young's business – like his ranch south of Provo that he visits now and again."

Jim's next question was not unexpected by the Ahernes, "Are you going to be a Mormon?"

"I don't know. I promised Mister Young I'd think about it and that I'd escort Laura to her church in Tacoma. I had to say that much before her father would agree to our marriage. Heck, I don't get to Mom's church that often. I'm not particularly religious, so how could I be a Mormon?"

Later that evening when everyone had retired early for a much-needed night's rest, the couple lay in bed and watched a gentle snowfall drift to earth through the open curtains. Nancy had a quirk for opening drapes or blinds following lights out, and Jim humored his wife because they were both early risers.

"Huh!" he said, blinking his eyes open to glance at Nancy.

"I said my brother must be in love the way he talks of church and marriage. He never has been a spiritual type," she whispered in a swall voice now that she had her husband's attention.

"Kind of like yours truly you mean. I believe Laura is less religious than her family if she agreed to marry Jack and live in Tacoma. I'm glad you agreed to be in their wedding, even if I can't go with you," Jim assayed.

"Oh, do you mind, Dear? I could stay home with you and the baby. Who'll we get to help you with our child? Dad was so pleased that you agreed to be 'Straw Boss' again he offered to pay for a nanny. He even complimented you when you went along with Jack to the tavern for a beer. He said, 'Josh Hill and Joe Hastings like your husband, and Edith told me it was peaceful and quiet with me gone. Can't you talk him into joining the family business?' Now that's high praise from everyone," Nancy's tone endorsed their positive opinions.

"Ha! Ha! everyone likes to be left alone at the warehouse, and I don't know enough to get in their way. Your Dad had a knack for hiring good people, you know," Jim reported and pecked her cheek as he concluded, "go to sleep. I have to get my rest if I'm going to be both boss and worker tomorrow."

*****

Wilhelm Edward Gerber was born on January 25, 1906 in the Aherne home, his presence announced demonstratively with a pair of healthy lungs. When Jim was allowed to hold his son and perch on the edge of his wife's bed, he thanked his lucky stars that both of his loved ones were doing so well. He even nodded agreement when Nancy queried, "Isn't Wilhelm beautiful? He'll be a handsome man one day – just like his father."

Jim kept his first thought private, lest he upset his happy sweetheart. *Nancy's a bit woozy from the delivery. I don't see how anyone can see beauty in this wrinkled little ragamuffin even though he's lovable. Hmm! My wife's euphoria has clouded her perception I'm afraid. Maybe he'll grow cuter with time.*

Aloud he declared, "He's our son and a strong lad. He'll be a fine young man, I'm sure. We'll see to it, my Dear! Now get some rest while I rock him to sleep."

*****

Whitecaps spewed salt spray into the air above the riptide as the Gerber family boat rounded Point Defiance. These discordant forces of nature pushed the fishing boat every which way as Jim revved his engine to control the wild winds, whirling eddies and constant rolling motion. Their progress was further impeded by fishermen at work and then a misty rain blowing into Jim's face.

Laura's humor came to fore as her husband frowned, his face showing worry wrinkles, "March is coming in like a lion and February hasn't exited yet. Cheer up, Dear, we'll be home in a few minutes."

Even as her effort was rewarded with a small smile on her husband's lips, the wind abated, and Jim relaxed and eased back on the throttle. He replied in kind, "Doggone it, Nancy, I brought our supplies out here yesterday without a riffle cracking the surface. Heck, I had time to catch a salmon for your Mom and still be home

for supper. I guess I should have delivered you and Will yesterday
and handled our supplies today. Wouldn't you know, Puget Sound
weather is always unpredictable at this time of year."

Nancy looked around as the rain let up, remarking, "Say,
what are those two men doing at the claybanks? Is someone going
to build down here?"

"Maybe. I heard Andrew Foss plans to build a boathouse
later in the year. Look, there's a couple of camps being built by our
cabin – more neighbors, I reckon," Jim observed, adding curiously,
"Do I see my son's eyes opening?"

"Probably, Will's been asleep the whole voyage. The boat
rocking seems to lull him into dreamland. I wish there was another child at camp. He'll be lonesome."

Jim grinned as he added, "And another woman would be
nice for you. All the old-timers are good neighbors but frugal con-
versationalists. They stand a bit in awe of a pretty lady."

"Why thank you, Husband of mine. I have noticed they talk
to you and listen to me. Hee! Hee! They make a good audience,"
Nancy teased as she waved her free hand toward their camp in concluding, "Speaking of company, they're waiting at the slip to help
us land."

*****

Life in camp during early spring was difficult for Nancy.
Baby Will claimed a lot of attention, and Jim was either fishing or
helping neighbors repair their cabins. As the March winds abated
and the air warmed along the Puget Sound, so was Will less
demanding. At least he slept all night and took his afternoon nap
without any fuss, and the tired mother slowly returned to her energetic self.

One stormy day a younger neighbor named Phil Strange
hiked up the bluff and through the woods to the settlement at the
company smelter, sometimes called Swansea but more often Rust's
Town, or just pain Ruston. He returned late in the afternoon with a
bottle of whiskey and a picnic hamper caging a live chicken.

As the fishermen gathered on the beach behind Gerbers'
cabin, Phil announced to all present, "If Missus Gerber will roast
this bird for us on Sunday, we'll have an Easter party. Can someone catch a salmon?"

"Phil, Easter was a couple of weeks ago, but I'll provide all
the salmon in my smokehouse if everyone else will bring some

spuds," Jim volunteered for his wife before whispering an aside, "You can roast a chicken, can't you?"

"Hee! Hee! No, but we'll learn together. We can't let our friends down, can we?"

Phil raised his hand like a boy in school and asked respectfully of Nancy, "And gravy, too? Is it all right for us bachelors to drink a little whiskey, ma'am?"

"Only if Jim and I get a shot as well. Now everyone gather your contributions to our feast and bring them to me. I only have two days to plan this feast," Nancy responded good-naturedly, wishing another woman lived at the Narrows. Company and help with the chores would be pleasant.

An hour later she thanked the men for the collection on her kitchen table, a bin of potatoes, a bag of flour and two tins of peaches. She ordered, "Jim your smoked salmon is wonderful for an hors d'oeuvre but I need a fresh salmon or two as well. That's your job!"

Phil blurted, "A what?" and blushed at his lack of knowledge.

Nancy blushed in turn, both of them laughing when she explained, "A bite of food to go with your whiskey so I have time to cook the meal."

Jim smiled and bobbed his head as he assented, "We'll all fish tomorrow, Dear. Did you hear Phil's idea?"

Nancy shook her head and glanced at their neighbor, who haltingly described his concept of a path to Ruston, "I marked a trail to town. It could be widened a bit but my real problem is this hillside behind us. I think we should build a walkway up the bluff, I mean a stairway like I saw in Ketchikan last..."

"Yah, and I might stay here all winter if I could get supplies without fighting a storm on the Narrows. Hmm, I bet they have a tavern in Ruston, too," another fellow remarked wistfully.

Before long everyone agreed to work on Monday, one old-timer admitting that he had been a carpenter in his youth, and then a second agreed to be his helper with a laconic admission, "I'll help here. Not much good at digging at my age."

At noon on Saturday Jim quit fishing and returned home to help Nancy, not at all optimistic in reporting, "Phil caught the only salmon in the Narrows. The rest of the fellas caught only dogfish. Let me clean up, and I'll watch Will until his nap."

Nancy grinned in relief as she replied, "Thank you, Dear. Our son seems to know something is going on – he's a pest. I'm going to knead my dough and let it rise overnight. Let's see if my biscuits are any good."

"Ha! Ha! Honey, these bachelors will eat anything and come back for more. I just hope someone catches another salmon."

With gray clouds swirling about, dusk settled about the Gerber cabin early. From out of the mist near the kelp bed came Phil's loud voice, "Jim Gerber, come help me. I have a treat for tomorrow's party."

Nancy was holding the baby so she watched curiously at their front window while Jim caught his friend's line and held his boat fast against the piling fenders. Spread over the bottom of Phil's boat was a monstrous octopus, fully five feet across and slapping tentacles about in an attempt to find freedom.

Phil boasted, "I bet she weighs twenty pounds Jim. I'm going to dress this beast out and prepare 'hors d'oeuvres' for your wife – octopus legs. Take that salmon away before this sea monster finds it."

Jim slipped his fingers under the salmon's gills and felt a sling rope-like appendage wrap around his wrist, leaving a pair of red circles on his skin as he reared back from the grip of it suckers. He heard Nancy squeal as she watched but ignored her alarm as he queried, "I've heard octopus are tasty, but isn't the meat tough as leather?"

Phil nodded sagely as he whispered *sotto voce*, "Yes, but I have an old fisherman's recipe for cooking it. You wait and see tomorrow."

His wife was adamant about letting any of that monster in the cabin, and Jim had to calm her down with a compromise, "Shush! Let's see what it tastes like after Phil fixes it. With one chicken and one salmon, we need all the appetizers we can get. I hear our two new neighbors are coming back tomorrow just to attend your party."

*****

By mid-morning Nancy and Jim had tasted bits of tenderized octopus dipped in a vinegar sauce, and the appetizer passed their test early. Naturally the neighbors gathered early to partake of Phil's special treat, the smoked salmon and Nancy's baking powder biscuits never making it to the dinner hour. Everyone took turns in holding the heavily-bundled baby until a light rain began to fall.

Nancy invited their guests inside, every square inch of the cabin floor covered with men, only the three really old-timers, Nancy and the holder of Will allowed a chair. The feast was a stupendous success even as Missus Gerber became simply "Nancy," that beautiful wife of "Lucky Jim" and their friend. Phil dubbed her the champion cook of the Narrows during the festivities.

The men's temperate drinking and well-mannered presence got them an invitation for lunch the next day while they built their walkway up the bluff. Jim and a half-dozen of the trail crew tested the pathway to Ruston when it was completed, replenishing their supplies with the little cash available. Fishing would improve with warmer spring weather, and money would be available when the salmon runs got started.

Will became a favorite of the camp bachelors although Jim claimed their neighbors just liked Nancy – and her baked bread and cookies. They would later recognize that spring was an idyllic time and one which encouraged them to think of year-round living at the Narrows.

Chapter 15

Smiling indulgently at his wife's restless behavior, Jim suggested, "Maybe we ought to catch this outgoing tide and go to Tacoma a day early."

Nancy's instant reply of "Yes" was accompanied by a grin and a question, "Am I that transparent, Dear?"

"Well, you have packed and unpacked Will's things twice in the last couple of days. You must be ready to leave our Narrows home. Are you excited about seeing Salt Lake City and the Young family? And being in the wedding?"

His wife's response came without a word as she handed Jim a bag of clean diapers, a second of baby clothing, and third of baby bottles and toys, "Load these in your boat, Daddy, and Will and I will dress for rainy weather."

"But the sun's shining," he jibed in riposte, both South Sounders knowing May still had a few showers to be expected.

*****

Grandma oohed and aahed over Will for several minutes before she abruptly remembered, "Oh yes, children. Mary Anderson offered to care for the baby while we're away. Jim, she suggested you both stay with her and Carl. Is that all right?"

Jim agreed quickly, "Of course! How generous of the Andersons. We'll spend the weekdays there and come here for the weekends, but I'll check the house every day on my way back from work."

"Could you stop by Jack's as well? He bought the place down the hill," Louise requested.

Nodding rapidly, Jim excused himself, "If that's settled, I'll tell Mary and go by the warehouse to visit with everyone. If Ed and Jack would like, I can begin work tomorrow. I expect they have a lot of errands to run before you all head for Utah."

Setting a brisk pace along Yakima Avenue, Jim passed the former college building on his way to the Andersons. No one answered the door so he left a note thanking Mary and Carl and announcing father and son would arrive day after tomorrow.

His route through downtown led him to Harry Maguire's office for a brief visit, and then he ambled over to his father-in-law's office. Ed and Jack both welcomed him and accepted his offer for tomorrow's substitution. His brother-in-law claimed his assistance right off, "Josh Hill and his warehouseman are home sick, and a load of freight was delivered. Ha! Ha! You're dressed just right to bring it inside, unpack the crates and stock the shelves. I need to go to the jewelry store."

"Don't look so smug, Jack, I like the work and a chance to visit everyone. I'll wear a tie tomorrow and play 'Boss.' You'd better get home early, your womenfolks are plotting in your absence. Tell Mom I'll be home for supper."

*****

Missus Hill sent word to the house that evening in the person of young Josh, her twelve-year old son, "Dad's very ill and can't work tomorrow."

Jim answered before Ed could comment, "Tell your Dad to get well, and I'll see him Monday." The boy grinned and ran home.

Responding to Ed's raised eyebrow, Jim chuckled under his breath as he said, "You wouldn't want Josh to spread his illness, would you? I'll take my work clothes along and help his new assistant when I have time. Relax and enjoy Salt Lake City and your son's wedding festivities."

He half expected his father-in-law would accompany him to work, but Ed just smiled and waved Jim out of the front door. Jim arrived early enough to look managerial, greeting employees and wandering around Ed's office – twiddling his thumbs so to speak.

Abruptly he stepped into the restroom and changed clothes, reveling in being busy as he got his hands dirty. He was pleased at the nods of approval from his colleagues, and was actually surprised at the number of people who tracked him down for an okay or word of advice. He wondered if Ed and Jack spent too much time in their offices, hands-on effort worked so well for him.

Aunt Edith was complimentary as they shared lunches at her desk upstairs, "Everyone thinks you're great helping the new warehouseman. Giving Josh extra sick leave made a good impression on his coworkers. My brother dispenses time off like a miser, but I think you're right, a healthy man is a productive employee."

"Isn't Ed always generous though?"

She nodded in support of her brother, but added, "He doles

it out like an autocrat. He seems to enjoy the control, but I believe he worries that someone might lie about being sick."

"Well, he could visit the employee at home. Or would that seem like snooping. Hmm, maybe I'll drop by the Hill's place and see if Josh needs any help," Jim concluded in uncertain tones.

Aunt Edith agreed, "Here! Take Josh a pulp magazine. He likes to read Ned Buntline's tales. And make sure he's getting good care. His wife is a good nurse probably, but he sounds very ill."

*****

Jim puffed short crisp breaths as he climbed Fifteenth Street with a Wild West pulp magazine in hand, the road leveling out as he reached J Street. He turned left and crossed the lane to a small but well-kept house with flowers growing by the front door. Stepping onto the porch with knuckles clenched to rap on the door, it opened to reveal a motherly woman in white dress and red-checkered apron. Her plain face was friendly as she asked, "Good afternoon. Can I help you?"

"Missus Hill?" produced a confirming nod as Jim continued, "I'm James Gerber, Ed Aherne's son-in-law. Is Josh well enough for a short visit?"

"Oh Mister Gerber, I should have recognized you from my husband's description," Gladys Hill greeted him with an attractive smile, her green eyes expressive. "Josh will be so glad to see you. He must be getting better since he's turned crusty with the children and me. Come in please."

Jim grinned in return and stepped across the sill, observing a neat and tidy household. A pretty girl of six or seven years stood in the kitchen doorway with her expression animated in curiosity even as she remained silent.

"I'm Gladys, and this is my daughter Melissa," she turned to the child as she spoke, "Missy, this man is Daddy's friend, Mister Gerber."

The girl nodded mutely as her mother explained, "Melissa is deaf, but she's smart even if she can't go to school. She reads lips."

Jim spoke slowly, enunciating clearly as Missus Hill had done, "Melissa is a pretty name. My name is James, or Jim. Momma used to call me J.K. when I was younger. My wife is Nancy Aherne, the daughter of our boss."

142 Royal LaPlante

Her muffled attempt to speak was not comprehensible, but from Gladys' expression of surprise it was unusual. Relying on his teaching experience, Jim smiled patiently and asked, "Can you say that again, Melissa? I'll listen better."

"DaDa sick...me help Momma," little Melissa struggled with the words and their pronunciation until her meaning was clear, and Jim nodded.

"I know Daddy is ill. Your brother Josh told me. Is your brother Josh Hill Junior?"

Melissa grinned in triumph. She was talking to the nice gentleman, so she spoke again with more confidence, "Yes, Josh and Bob go to school. Er...you read?"

Raising the magazine so she could see the cover, Jim admitted, "Yes, I am a teacher. These stories are a gift for your Daddy. Can you read?"

The child's smile vanished in a nonce, and she turned glum – and mute. Her mother understood her daughter well, however, and insisted, "Missy be good. Answer Mister Gerber."

Jim was about to overlook her behavior, then thought the better of it, Missus Hill seemed to know what she was doing.

Melissa's eyes had a woebegone expression, but she was obedient as she blurted, "No,...," her tears obscuring her words.

"Melissa, don't you go to school?" Jim queried.

"No! stupid...no read."

"You are not stupid, Melissa. I think you are smart and could learn to read. It is hard when you can't hear, but you speak well when you try. I'm glad to meet you."

Missus Hill asked, "Missy, will you finish the dishes please? I hear Daddy fussing. I'm sure he wants to talk to Mister Gerber."

To Jim she simply beckoned him into a short hallway with a "Follow me!" She led him to their bedroom where Josh was propping himself up on his elbows and two pillows and croaking out an apology, "I'm sorry I can't talk much, Jim. Will you tell me the news from the warehouse?"

"You're looking strong enough, Josh. By Monday you'll be in shape to tell your new warehouseman how to do his job. Here's a magazine to read, Ned Buntline stories will pass the time."

Josh coughed to clear his throat and teased Jim, "You worked today, eh? Ed's got you all dressed up I see. Have the Ahernes gone to Salt Lake City already?"

"No, not till tomorrow. This time I took my work clothes to the office and taught your man to handle freight properly. Thought I'd better wear my tie and collar home to impress my father-in-law," Jim chattered along.

"I know, Jim, you're just one of us in the warehouse. I wish you'd take Ed up on his offer. You're a good boss," Josh offered some simple advice.

"Thanks, Josh, but I love fishing from our Narrows cabin. I'm my own boss. However, I did promise to fill in for Jack over the Christmas holidays. I reckon he's going to Salt Lake City with Laura," Jim stated informatively as he turned to the hallway.

"Good! Thanks for visiting and bringing something to read. I'll see you Monday."

*****

The following three weeks passed swiftly, Nancy and her family traveling to Utah, Mary Anderson "adopting" baby Will as a pseudo-grandson, and Jim balancing his time between fatherhood and warehouse management. He divided his days between the Andersons' home when working and the Aherne mansion on week-ends. His son didn't seem to care which house was which as long as DaDa was around. Of course Carl didn't have the fine ear to hear Will's "DaDa" properly, but Jim swore he said it nonetheless.

One unbusy day in late May Jim took time off to walk all the way to the College of Puget Sound. Ostensibly he was visiting the new campus, but Jim had a question for his friend, Professor Smith. Was there a school in Tacoma where young Melissa Hill could learn to read?

James Smith greeted his former student warmly, showing him around the campus and ending up in Ben Adam's classroom. The Adams family had a boy who was deaf and getting an education. Professor Adams gave Jim the name and address of a tutor who might help Melissa but warned that the woman instructor charged a fair price.

Jim walked back the way he had come with a rosy glow of friendship and a sentimental feeling for the college. On reaching K Street he began searching for Sarah Lowell's house number, finally stopping before a butcher shop with the name John Lowell, Proprietor, etched in the window. A door to the side of the establishment was obviously the Lowells' living quarters, and Jim entered a small foyer to climb the stairwell to the second floor.

Rapping sharply, Jim stepped back to wait for the door to open, a schoolmarm-looking woman of thirty years or so soon greeting him, "Good day, sir. Can I help you?"

Jim smiled and replied, "I hope so. I'm seeking Sarah Lowell, a tutor who Professor Ben Adams recommended."

"Oh, one of Doctor Adams' friends. His nephew is one of my pupils. Do you have a deaf child?" Sarah asked as she led him to her study where a girl of ten years sat at a school desk, one of three in the room.

"Abigail, keep working. I'll return in a few minutes to check your work," the tutor instructed, receiving no visible acknowledgement from the young girl.

Once they were seated nearby in the parlor, Jim introduced himself, "I'm James Gerber. I don't have a deaf child but a friend does. Her name is Melissa Hill, she's six years old and reads lips fairly well but wants to read better. She's as intelligent as any child I've taught."

"Oh, you're a teacher. Where?"

Jim shook his head and explained, "I've taught grammar school at Gig Harbor and Point Fosdick, but right now I'm helping my wife's family with their business. Ed Aherne is my father-in-law. Most of the time I live at the Narrows and fish for a living. Can you help my friend Melissa?"

Sarah smiled her encouragement and offered, "I'd love the challenge if your opinion is correct. You know, many parents can't afford to pay my fee, and often those people who are well-to-do send their children to boarding school."

Jim nodded in understanding as he replied, "Thanks for answering my questions. I'll talk to the Hills, and they can discuss their situation with you."

*****

The following week Josh confided in Jim that the family wanted to send Missy to Missus Lowell, but they were short on cash, and then invited him to Sunday dinner, "Gladys wants your opinion after she talked to that tutor. Bring Will along, and my Missus will feed us her roast beef special."

"Is two o'clock a good time to visit?"

Josh nodded agreeably, leaving the office to run an errand for Aunt Edith. As soon as he walked out the door, Jim motioned

Joe Hastings to his office for a conference, asking a tactful question, "Joe, would you give me a little advice?"

"Of course, Jim! Is anything wrong?" he answered quickly.

Jim grinned at the idea as he asserted, "No, but I have a concern for Josh. Do you know his daughter Melissa is deaf?"

Joe was a bit taken aback at the question, hesitating a moment before replying, "Yes I do. Melissa is a bright girl – even talks a little. Why do you ask?"

"Melissa needs to be tutored, but it costs more than the Hills can pay. I wondered if Ed ever gives a bonus. Do I have the authority? Be frank Joe, I don't want to put you on the spot," Jim stated as diplomatically as possible.

"Oh I see, Jim. Well, only Ed can change salaries, including bonuses. Let me read my instructions and chat with Edith – no offense intended, Boss," Hastings concluded, rushing to his desk for a paper and then running up the stairs to visit Aunt Edith.

Jim busied himself signing letters and initializing shipment orders, not paying much attention to the constant movement of his fellow workers. He rose to don his jacket a few moments after closure only to find no one had gone home. The entire crew was standing before his office door, his quizzical expression eliciting only solemn faces.

Joe Hastings bustled forward, his wide grin echoed by everyone on the floor as he announced, "Jim, Edith and I passed the hat for Josh's Melissa. Maybe Ed will give our friend a bonus, but we can't wait. Here!"

Jim was offered a leather purse jingling with coins, and his glance went around to every eye as he dug deeply into his pocket for his only money, a five-dollar gold piece. Dropping it into the proffered purse, he raised his voice to declare, "Thank you one and all my friends. Joe always finds a great solution when I give him a problem. He can carry all this cash over to the Hills with me – a gift from their friends at Aherne's."

A cheer went up with several men and women stopping to congratulate both messengers as the employees headed home. Aunt Edith in her wheelchair was last to leave, and she suggested, "We'll work on my brother for a bonus as well, Jim. By the way, everyone told me that you should take up on his offer to work here. You are a popular Straw Boss."

"Ha! Ha! I'll twist Ed's arm for Melissa but it's fishing for me next month. Good night, Aunt Edith," Jim leaned over to kiss her forehead in affection as she left. His errant thought was, *Nancy's kin are nice people – even Jack I guess.*

To Joe he ordered, "Well, come along, Paymaster. We'll go to Hill's home and tell him his friends want Melissa to learn to read." The Straw Boss grinned happily as the excited and chattering Mister Hastings matched him stride for stride up the hill to J Street and over to the Hill's place.

In fact, the presentation was a bit of a letdown for Jim after Joe's energetic display, but the look on the girl's face was enough of a reward when her Daddy told her she was going to school with Missus Lowell.

*****

Jim took to Laura the day the newlyweds returned from Salt Lake City. Jack's outspoken criticism of a bonus for Josh Hill was countered by the bride out of hand, with Ed's quick agreement cementing Jim's suggestion. Melissa Hill's schooling became an Aherne project, even the frowning son finally acceding to family pressure.

The Gerbers stayed over an extra couple of days to help Jack and Laura open their first home, with Jim spending time in the warehouse until Jack was ready to return to work, as Vice-President no less.

Finally the day came when Grandma had to give up her darling Willie so the fishing family could resume their life at the Narrows. Both Jim and Nancy were excitedly looking forward to summer in their Narrows Camp.

Chapter 16

Warm sunny days followed the Fourth of July, and salmon fishing was successful for all the beach residents. Will was hale and hearty enough that his demanding appetite required weekly trips to Ruston over that new trail. Milk and cream, plus vegetables and fruit improved the family diet as well as the baby's. Their son was especially fond of mashed potatoes and bananas, the latter a rare treat only available at the market now and then.

Plodding up the hillside trail one morning, he heard his name called, "Hey Jim, wait up. I'll walk to Ruston with you." Phil vaulted up the wooden stairs two at a time to join his neighbor on the sandy path, grinning widely as he whispered sotto voce, "I'm going to buy a chicken. Do you think Nancy will roast it for me?"

"Ha! Ha! You should ask her I reckon. I tell you what, I'll buy one, too. She can't say 'no' to both of us, can she? I've got a pair of silvers in my fish box, but nothing in my smokehouse," Jim rejoindered in planning another summer party. He thought they might be starting a tradition for the Narrows residents.

The next day every neighbor brought some item of food to the Gerber cabin, Nancy accepting the food and visiting with each man. Jim tended his son and worried about their lack of smoked salmon, pleasantly surprised when a boat putted up to their landing with Puyallup Harry's family – and a gunny sack of smoked salmon. His friend was apologetic about butting in on their party but was silenced the moment Nancy and Annie started cooking. Their husbands welcomed the task of fixing hors d'oeuvres while Phil played with Will and little Annie.

As in the previous summer, a bottle was passed around while the men ate cheese, biscuits and smoked salmon. Annie fretted visibly, her signals to Harry ignored. Nancy finally whispered to Jim, "Our friend is a true Indian, Dear. He can't handle whiskey."

Always ready with a plausible solution, Jim faced this problem directly. He drank a lion's share of Harry's liquor when the Puyallup wasn't looking. Nancy shrugged her shoulders and grinned wryly. She knew the two friends would be equally tipsy before the afternoon was over.

The wives threw a blanket over the snoring forms of their men and cleaned up the remnants of their successful party even as their last guests started home.

*****

Jim and Harry fished together for two days while the women visited and prepared a picnic meal. Both families sailed to Gig Harbor to sell their fish and buy a ham for their basket, moving on to Owens Beach near Point Defiance for their picnic feast.

Coincidentally an old acquaintance showed up at their fire, Fred Owens was eating with several Indians at a nearby campfire. He greeted them in a friendly manner, "Hello, folks! Jim, Nancy, Harry, Annie – and your children?"

"Yes, Fred. It's good to see you again. Meet Will and Little Annie. How are things at Point Fosdick?"

"Just fine, Jim, except our new teacher wrote me that he'll be late for the school term. I bet he's fishing in Alaska. Would you consider teaching his class for a few days in September? Maybe a week?" Fred asked imploringly.

"Be glad to help out, Fred. Let me know for sure before school starts. My family is living at the Narrows. Now tell us whether the Owens family owns this beach or not," Jim teased, knowing full well that there was no connection between his friend and Owens Beach. He was looking forward to hearing Fred's tall tale once again, sure the others would enjoy the entertaining tale.

*****

A sailing yacht carried the Aherne family to the Gerber cabin in late August to see Nancy's home and the Narrows, catch a salmon or two, and confirm Jim's promise to work when Jack and Laura went to Utah in mid-December. It was a pleasant interlude for everyone, especially for Nancy. Jim felt comfortable about leaving her for a few days to teach at the Point Fosdick Reservation School.

Ed pointed to the Foss Boathouse down the beach, commenting, "Andrew said his family was building here. When will it be finished?"

"They're pretty much done for this summer Ed, but they'll be adding an activity center next year I hear. We hope it'll include a grocery store as well. Living here year-round might be possible with a few amenities. Several fishermen have tried spending the winter, but each man has given up – Christmas and stormy weather have discouraged everyone."

The grandparents opted to visit with Will after lunch, so Jim took Jack and Laura fishing for salmon, an incoming tide allowing their borrowed yacht to rest at anchor offshore. His sister-in-law demonstrated her warm and lively personality when she caught a twenty-pound Chinook, her shrieks, laughter and even a gentlewoman's curse echoing off the bluff. Jim gained new appreciation for Jack's wife and thought him a lucky fellow indeed.

*****

The fall season passed without incident, fishing producing a sizeable hoard of income to be deposited in their savings account at the Tacoma Bank. Nancy complained about leaving their Narrows cabin, "I love our home, Dear, and even the Christmas visit to my parents isn't as good as being here. With our savings growing, maybe we can start living here year-round. Will likes it, too. He's spending a lot of time watching storms out the front window."

Jim grinned as he agreed, "Me, too! I won't promise Jack any help next year. We'll just go to your folks on Christmas Eve for two days."

Will gurgled happily, so Jim added, "See, our son loves his home, too."

The Gerbers' stay at the Ahernes for a month was bright with family events, friendly with visits to the Andersons, the Behrings and the guys at Puget Sound Freight. They also attended a party at the warehouse and chatted with Aunt Edith, who doted on her grand-nephew while Jim listened to Melissa Hill read from her primer. Finally they took a walking tour of the College of Puget Sound and spent an hour with Professor Smith.

New Year 1907 arrived in no time, the Gerber family doubly pleased when they were free to return home, and Nancy learned she was with child again, the blessed event anticipated in mid-July. It seemed that the South Sound and the Narrows Camp were growing in population, and the Gerbers were happy with their lot.

Epilogue

The Tacoma Narrows is the waterway into the South Sound and the cultural heritage of the Nisqually, Squaxin and Puyallup Indians. European exploration failed to disturb their lives until the late eighteenth century when Peter Puget passed through the restricted waters of the Narrows.

The Northwest experienced a heated rivalry for the flourishing fur trade coveted by both the United States and Great Britain during the following fifty years. Fort Vancouver was built on the Columbia River in 1825 with Fort Nisqually added to the Hudson Bay Company expansion in 1833. Oregon Trail pioneers and California Forty-Niners came west by the thousands in mid-century, settlers and prospectors far outnumbering British fur traders. The Wilkes Expedition of 1841 and the establishment of Fort Steilacoom in 1849 subverted British power in the Puget Sound.

Washington Territory split from Oregon Territory in 1852, and its northern boundary moved with the continued influx of Yankees, until the 1859 Pig War in the San Juan Islands resulted in the present-day Canadian-American border.

North of Steilacoom, Lemon Beach, Day Island and Titlow Beach, the bluffs rose high and only a thin gravelly shelf extended into the powerful currents of the Narrows. In 1883 Charles C. Miller purchased 128.90 acres of land along the Tacoma shoreline, his territorial title challenged when Washington became a state in 1889. The Narrows Realty Company eventually gained title to that tract and more land in West Tacoma.

Fishermen from Steilacoom to Wollochet Bay to Gig Harbor began squatting along the beach in rudimentary shanties as early as 1903, using the Narrows Camps as a fishing base during the summer months.

Andrew and Thea Foss expanded their Commencement Bay rental rowboat business into harbor tugs (Foss Maritime Corporation) and a second boathouse at the Tacoma Narrows in 1906. Fishermen's shacks took on a sturdier look as a small village evolved about the Foss Boathouse, and the path to Ruston developed into a rough roadway. In 1908 the first family resided year-round, giving the Narrows Camps a more permanent status. Foss built a clubhouse in 1913, and Charles Zeigler made it into a general store known as the Salmon Beach Grocery in 1915. This romantic village within a city still flourishes a century later.

The University of Puget Sound occupied a temporary location at Eighth Street and Yakima Avenue at the turn of the century, moving to Sixth Avenue and Sprague Street in 1904 and becoming the College of Puget Sound until 1923 (present-day site of Jason Lee Middle School). Ever in the need for more land for expansion, college officials looked at the undeveloped west end of Tacoma near Lemon Beach. Narrows Realty Company named a tract of its proposed development, "University Place," but the College of Puget Sound selected a north end campus site at Fifteenth and Warner Streets. The University of Puget Sound is still expanding its programs and facilities as an institution of higher learning on this same site.

Recognizing the tremendous potential of the Puget Sound region as Washington Territory split off from Oregon Territory in 1852, government leaders including Isaac Stevens selected the South Sound's largest village (250 people) to be its capital. Walla Walla was much larger but on the wrong side of the Cascade Mountains, while the other small settlements of Tacoma, Seattle, Bellingham and Port Townsend were passed over.

To this list of real people and events described in Puget Sound history books, the reader should add Chief Leschi and his brother Quiemuth of the Nisquallies. Other Indian characters join Jim Gerber, his family, friends and occasional foes in the author's fictionalized version of the period.

Historical Perspectives

Great Britain sent Captain George Vancouver to the Pacific coast of North America to explore and to lay claim to its territory for the Crown. He entered the Strait of Juan de Fuca in the spring of 1792, continuing into the labyrinth of passages, bays and islands of a great inland waterway. He met many local Indians as he studied the new territory, diplomatically fostering friendly relations with the Native Americans. One example noted in his journal was a feast with the Puyallups on Caledonia Beach, just north of a large bay which Vancouver described in some detail, as yet unnamed Commencement Bay.

Burdened with a multitude of tasks, Vancouver sent Lieutenant Peter Puget with a small party in the ship's gig to survey the southern reaches of what the Captain eventually named "Puget Sound."

The Hudson Bay Company established a network of fur trading posts or forts across the continent, and Vancouver's seaports became an extension of that enterprise. Fort Vancouver became a major center of fur trade and commerce – a symbol of British power in the Northwest. To the south Fort Umpqua was an important arm of HBC rule, and in 1833 Fort Nisqually was built on Sequalitchew Creek near present day Dupont on the Puget Sound. The British claim to the Northwest was firmly established.

The United States of America had similar goals to expand across the continent, Lewis and Clark exploring the Columbia River after the Louisiana Purchase was completed. Yankees had an irrepressible habit of ignoring British boundary lines, and their numbers far outstripped HBC fur traders. Soon the British claims changed to all land north of the Columbia River.

In 1841, Lieutenant Charles Wilkes commanded a United States naval vessel on its visit to the Puget Sound. Within the shadow of Fort Nisqually, Wilkes surveyed and named several places such as Gig Harbor and Commencement Bay. He left the indelible stamp of American expansionism.

During the following decade, a flood of Yankees moved into Puget Sound, the Oregon Trail and Natches Pass routes, admitting Americans in ever-increasing numbers, including George

Bush, a Negro settler excluded from Oregon because of his race. Bush moved into Olympia in 1845 with Sawyers Simmons and Delin, the latter setting up his sawmill in 1852 at the foot of Gallihan's Gulch near present-day Twenty-sixth Street and Puyallup Avenue in Tacoma. During this period Job Carr built his log cabin on the shore of Commencement Bay, lumber becoming a backbone of the economy at Commencement City.

British authority atrophied as the Hudson Bay Company gave up its forts. The United States built Fort Steilacoom in 1849, supplanting nearby Fort Nisqually. The following years led to Steilacoom being the first incorporated town on Puget Sound in 1854, and the Thomas Chambers Mill built on the estuary of the creek named after him being a fine example of prosperity for Steilacoom and Pierce County.

It was during this period that a brief-lived Indian War broke out following the Treaty of Medicine Creek, a tributary of the Nisqually River located halfway between Fort Steilacoom and Washington's territorial capital of Olympia.

Chief Leschi of the Nisqually Tribe refused to cede his tribal land and sign the treaty. Governor Isaac Stevens sent federal marshals with orders to escort Leschi to his office, but the Nisqually Chief refused to go. Within days fighting broke out in rural Pierce County, organized Indian raids causing strife from Seattle's Alki Point to Olympia. The citizens around Delin's mill on Commencement Bay fled to safety within the walls of Fort Steilacoom. By the time U.S. Army troops reached the fort and were deployed, much of the fight had gone out of the Indians and peace returned to the South Sound.

Weeks after the fighting was over Chief Leschi naively ventured into the Sutler's Store at Fort Steilacoom, leisurely shopping in a familiar manner. The authorities were notified and the Nisqually Chief was arrested, tried for murder, and then hung within a year. It was one of the few times that a defeated War Chief was executed for defending his tribal lands.

An anomaly of treaty diplomacy in Washington Territory is evident even in modern times. Those tribes which ignored Governor Isaac Stevens' "peace treaties", and failed to acknowledge United States sovereignty over the territory became nonexistent. Their people were never on record and had no rights as a "tribe." Examples include the Meshai, who exist as a clan of the Nisqually; and in Skagit Valley, the Sauk and Suiattle who are classified as Skagits.

As Washington Territory developed following the American Civil War, Commencement City became Tacoma, its name derived from majestic "Tahoma" revered by the local Indians. Mount Tahoma was renamed by George Vancouver for his friend and supporter Rainier, but local old-timers often call it by its native appellation.

With the closure of Fort Steilacoom in 1868, the town's glory days faded into the past. In 1880 Tacoma became county seat as well as the industrial heart of the South Sound.

Lumber was king in the Puget Sound's early days and remained so for Tacoma in the decades to come. A score of sawmills lined the shoreline from the City Waterway to Point Defiance, the federal military reservation on that site converted into a major city park. The City of Destiny has maintained Point Defiance Park as a natural forest as well as tourist attraction ever since.

Part of the territory's growth was achieved by cheap labor imported from China. Smugglers brought the itinerant workers into Puget Sound and specifically Tacoma in spite of immigration control, using imaginative methods of entrance such as Chinese tunnels. It seemed that every underground conduit built for sewer, electric lines or other useful purpose was thought to be originally a smugglers' tunnel. Myths abounded for the century to come.

Common sobriquets of Coolie, Celestial, Chink and Oriental were expressions of prejudice used in reference to Chinese laborers. Hatred and bigotry resulted in the infamous Chinese expulsion in 1885, gangs of vigilantes driving every Chinese immigrant out of Tacoma and then burning their homes in Chinatown to the ground so none would try to return.

A territorial government investigation of the one-day incident proved to be fruitless, rumors abounding to the effect that Tacoma City leaders were criminally involved were widely believed. For decades to come the Chinese avoided Tacoma.

The Northern Pacific Railroad reached its western terminus in Tacoma in 1887, producing a boon in conjunction with several industrial barons, notably Lumberman Morton Matthew McCarver of "Old Tacoma," towboatman Andrew Foss of City Waterway (Thea Foss Waterway today), and Smelter magnate William Rust of Ruston. Tacoma grew prosperous with its port, railway, lumber and industry.

Puget Sound communities were producing dynamic results with growth of cities, industries and financial strength, earning Washington its statehood in 1889.